LAKE THIRTEEN

Reviewers Love Greg Herren's Mysteries

"Herren, a loyal New Orleans resident, paints a brilliant portrait of the recovering city, including insights into its tight-knit gay community. This latest installment in a powerful series is sure to delight old fans and attract new ones."—*Publishers Weekly*

"Fast-moving and entertaining, evoking the Quarter and its gay scene in a sweet, funny, action-packed way."—*New Orleans Times-Picayune*

"Herren does a fine job of moving the story along, deftly juggling the murder investigation and the intricate relationships while maintaining several running subjects."—*Echo* Magazine

"An entertaining read."—*OutSmart* Magazine

"A pleasant addition to your beach bag."—*Bay Windows*

"Greg Herren gives readers a tantalizing glimpse of New Orleans." —*Midwest Book Review*

"Herren's characters, dialogue and setting make the book seem absolutely real."—*The Houston Voice*

"So much fun it should be thrown from Mardi Gras floats!" —*New Orleans Times-Picayune*

"Greg Herren just keeps getting better."—*Lambda Book Report*

Praise for *Greg Herren's YA novels*

"Herren is to be lauded, not just for his contributions to the mystery genre, but for his prolific nature and the genuinely high quality of his output. It seems no matter what he tries, he finds success. Try Sara and see if you don't agree."—Jerry Wheeler, *Out in Print*

Timothy "is a sure and confident classic Herren page-turner and I can't image anyone not enjoying it late past their bedtime." —Lambda Literary

"Greg Herren is a master storyteller, and his latest book is no exception. [Sleeping Angel] is a beautifully crafted mystery, geared to a young adult audience, with a focus on family and peer relationships and a valuable lesson about tolerance. It's strongly recommended reading for teens…5 stars out of 5 stars"—Bob Lind, *Echo Magazine*

"This fast-paced mystery is skillfully crafted. Red herrings abound and will keep readers on their toes until the very end. Before the accident, few readers would care about Eric, but his loss of memory gives him a chance to experience dramatic growth, and the end result is a sympathetic character embroiled in a dangerous quest for truth."—*VOYA*

Sleeping Angel "will probably be put on the young adult (YA) shelf, but the fact is that it's a cracking good mystery that general readers will enjoy as well. It just happens to be about teens…A unique viewpoint, a solid mystery and good characterization all conspire to make *Sleeping Angel* a welcome addition to any shelf, no matter where the bookstores stock it."—Jerry Wheeler, *Out in Print*

By The Author

The Scotty Bradley Adventures
Bourbon Street Blues
Jackson Square Jazz
Mardi Gras Mambo
Vieux Carré Voodoo
Who Dat Whodunnit

The Chanse MacLeod Mysteries
Murder in the Rue Dauphine
Murder in the Rue St. Ann
Murder in the Rue Chartres
Murder in the Rue Ursulines
Murder in the Garden District
Murder in the Irish Channel

Sleeping Angel
Sara
Timothy
Lake Thirteen

Women of the Mean Streets
Men of the Mean Streets
Night Shadows
(edited with J. M. Redmann)

LAKE THIRTEEN

by

Greg Herren

2013

LAKE THIRTEEN
© 2013 BY GREG HERREN. ALL RIGHTS RESERVED.

ISBN 10: 1-60282-894-6
ISBN 13: 978-1-60282-894-0

THIS TRADE PAPERBACK ORIGINAL IS PUBLISHED BY
BOLD STROKES BOOKS, INC.
P.O. BOX 249
VALLEY FALLS, NY 12185

FIRST EDITION: AUGUST 2013

CREDITS
EDITOR: RUTH STERNGLANTZ
PRODUCTION DESIGN: SUSAN RAMUNDO
COVER DESIGN BY SHERI (GRAPHICARTIST2020@HOTMAIL.COM)

Acknowledgments

In August of 2011, I attended a writer's retreat for Bold Strokes Books authors at the Garnet Hill Lodge in upstate New York. In that serene country setting, the idea for *Lake Thirteen* came to me. So, first of all, I have to thank everyone at Bold Strokes Books who worked on putting the retreat together, because there would be no book without the retreat.

I also had a wonderful time there, hanging out with and exploring the woods and going ghost hunting with what I have come to refer to as the Beaver Pond Gang: Carsen Taite, Nell Stark, Trinity Tam, Anne Laughlin, Rachel Spangler, Lisa Girolami, Karis Walsh, Lynda Sandoval, Niner Baxter, Linda Braasch, and the wonderful Ruth Sternglantz. (If I forgot anyone, my apologies. I'm getting old.)

Ruth Sternglantz was my editor for *Lake Thirteen,* and made it an absolutely amazing experience. Thanks, Ruthie, I love you!

The behind the scenes people at Bold Strokes rock pretty hard too: Sandy Lowe, Cindy Cresap, Stacia Seaman, and everyone else are so infinitely patient and don't mind my forgetting deadlines or never knowing which book they're talking about when they contact me with a question.

My co-workers at the NO/AIDS Task Force not only do good work, but are a lot of fun to spend time with: Josh Fegley, the Evil Mark Drake, Brandon Benson, Matthew Valletta, Alex Leigh, Drew Davenport, Lauren Gauthier, Aaron Moses, Joey Bean, Larry Stillings, Nick Parr, Tim Kinzel, Matt Reese, and everyone in the Prevention Department.

My New Orleans support base are the best: Julie Smith, Lee Pryor, Pat Brady, Michael Ledet, Bev and Butch Marshall, Konstantine Smorodnikov, Lisa Anderson, Karissa Kary, Billy Martin, Ked Dixon, Todd Perley, Susan Larson, the Duvals (thanks for the LSU tickets, always!), Chris Wiltz, Nevada Barr, Don Paxton, the gang at Garden District Books (Amy, Ted, Britton), Jean Redmann, Gillian Rodger, Allison Vertovec, and Jesse and Laura Ledet. Love you guys!

Martin Strickland, Meghan Davidson, Robin Pearce, and Daniella Rivera: I still miss you guys. Move back!

Radclyffe has been an absolute dream to work for: thank you so much, Boss!

And of course, my dear friends all over the country: Stephen Driscoll, Stuart Wamsley, Victoria A. Brownworth, Rob Byrnes, Becky Cochrane, Timothy J. Lambert, Jess Wells, Michele Karlsberg, Kelly Smith, Val McDermid, Marianne Martin, Amie E. Evans, Lindsay Smolensky, Rhonda Rubin, the gang at Murder by the Book in Houston, everyone on the board at Mystery Writers of America, Jeffrey Ricker, 'Nathan and Dan Smith, Mike Smid, Kara Keegan, Dawn Lobaugh, Felice Picano, Trebor Healey, and Carol Rosenfeld: I couldn't ask for a more motley crew.

I can always count on the "board" to have my back. Love y'all.

And of course, Paul Willis, the foundation my life is built upon. I love you.

Dedication

This is for the Beaver Pond Gang with all my heart

CHAPTER ONE

A re you listening to me, Scotty?"
My mom's voice was so loud, I almost dropped my cell phone. I looked up. She was smiling at me in the space between the two front seats of the rental Subaru Forester, but her eyes meant business.

"Seriously," she went on, her smile never wavering, "if you're going to spend the whole week staring at your phone or fiddling with it, I'll just take it away from you now." She held out her right hand, palm up. "I'm not joking."

I looked at the screen of my phone and sighed before slipping it into my shorts pocket. I smiled back at her. "There, happy?"

"It's only a week," she said before turning back around. "You'll live, trust me."

Easy for you to say, I thought, turning to look out the window. It was still raining. It was raining when our flight from Chicago landed in Albany and hadn't let up for even a minute as we headed north. I pressed my forehead against the rain-spattered glass as the GPS gave my dad another direction and he headed up an off-ramp.

"It's only about another half hour," my dad said as he came to a stop at the top of the ramp, turning on his left-turn signal. He looked at me in the rearview mirror. "You're not still nervous, are you?"

I bit my lower lip and didn't respond.

"I think you're worrying for nothing," Mom said. "Nancy and Jerry and Lynda and David raised their kids right, just like we did with you."

Easy for you to say, I thought, looking out the back window at the two other rental cars following us. *You're not gay, and you didn't just come out to them all in an e-mail.*

We'd been taking these joint family vacations my entire life—I couldn't remember a summer when our three families *hadn't* taken one of these trips together. When we were kids, we'd shared a cousin-like camaraderie and looked forward to seeing each other every summer. But now that we were teens, we were like five strangers with a shared past. The last few years, it seemed to take a few days before everyone stopped sulking about having to come and decided to make the best of the situation. By the end of the week, the old bonds would be strongly and firmly in place again, and there would be sad good-byes at the airport. For about a week or so after, there would be a lot of texting and e-mailing. Once we settled back into our real lives and routines again, the contact became rarer. Within a month it died down again to an occasional comment on Facebook.

I was an only child, so it always seemed like I looked forward to the reunion more than the other four.

This year was different, though. This year, I'd dreaded coming, hadn't wanted to leave our nice suburb of Chicago and spend a week with four almost-strangers my own age.

All I knew about their lives was gleaned from Facebook, which was hardly the best source for personal information.

One would never know from looking at *my* Facebook page, for example, that I was gay.

I'd come out to my parents at the beginning of the summer. It hadn't been easy, but it was getting harder and harder to keep it from them, to keep lying to them. So, finally, one night at dinner I told them. They took it really well—I knew from talking to other gay teens in online chat rooms that some parents disowned their gay kids, going as far as throwing them out, but I'd been pretty sure my parents weren't like that. They weren't thrilled—I could see my mother was seeing her dreams of being a grandmother going out the window—but they weren't disappointed in *me*. Their primary concern was I wait to come out publicly until I was in college. They were worried I'd be bullied.

Besides, Marc just wasn't ready to take that step now, and if I came out, well, it would pretty much out him, too. I was lucky—I had cool parents. Marc's dad was horrible, just the kind of man who would throw his son out for being gay without a second thought. And I was lucky to have Marc, even if Marc wasn't ready to be as open as I wanted to be. So many of the queer kids I met online felt alone, wanting to fall in love but not knowing where they could meet someone, and I had the perfect guy living right down the street.

But I wanted to come out to my oldest friends, the kids who were like family to me. I must have drafted that e-mail a thousand times, almost pressing send, but then saving the draft when I chickened out. Finally, I sent it, earlier this week.

Not one of them responded.

Not one.

They'd all seemed okay with me at the airport in Albany, though.

I felt my phone vibrate in my pocket and carefully slid it back out. Keeping an eye on my mother, I checked the screen and smiled. *Hang in there you'll be home before you know it.*

I sighed with relief and looked back out the window. Dad had slowed to drive through a town that was barely visible through the downpour. "Almost there," he said cheerfully. "This is North Hollow, and according to the directions, Thirteenth Lake Road is just beyond the town limits."

"Doesn't look like much of a town," I said.

"The main part of the town isn't on this road," Mom replied. "There should be a turnoff up here that's the main street. According to what I found online, there are some great antique shops and little cafés and restaurants in North Hollow."

I smothered a grin. Mom had her own web-design business and worked at home. One of my teachers once referred to her "ruthless efficiency," and it was probably the best description of her I'd ever heard. She *was* ruthlessly efficient. The house was always spotless, we never seemed to run out of anything, and she never seemed tired. Her cooking was the envy of all my friends, and she always found the time to make it to all of my tennis matches and every choir or play performance I was in. Anytime we took a trip, she researched everything possible about the area—she had a folder in her shoulder bag with brochures, maps, and information about the part of upstate New York we were visiting.

"I hope it isn't going to rain all week," she went on. "We won't be able to do *anything*—and I can't imagine any worse hell than being trapped indoors with five bored teenagers for a week."

"It wouldn't dare rain," Dad replied. "It's supposed to be sunny all week." He started slowing down and leaned forward, peering through the windshield as the GPS announced, "Left turn in five hundred feet."

I turned and looked out the window. Now that we'd passed the town, the road was running alongside the Hudson River. There were whitecaps out there in the water.

"There it is," Dad said, "Thirteenth Lake Road." He put on his blinker and took the left turn slowly and smoothly. The Forester started climbing up the steep road.

Mohawk Lodge and Resort was on the side of a small mountain, I knew that much, and on the shores of Lake Thirteen. There were a lot of lakes in this region, and the lodge was about an hour's drive from Lake George. Dad slowed down as the rain started coming down harder, and in the distance lightning flashed, followed shortly by the roar of thunder.

"Approaching destination," the GPS announced. "Prepare for arrival."

"That doesn't make sense," Mom said, and she bent down to start digging through her bag.

"You have arrived at destination."

I leaned forward, looking through the windshield. There was a road to the right, and Dad turned on his signal. I could barely make out the street sign, but the road was marked Cemetery Road.

I felt a chill as Dad stopped the car and put it in park. I looked out the back again and saw the other two cars parked along the side of the road behind us. There was forest on both sides of Cemetery Road. Dad's phone started ringing, and he pulled it out of the drink holder in between the two front seats to answer it. "Hello, David.

Yeah, the GPS is messed up. It says this is where the lodge is, but I know it's not on Cemetery Road."

"It isn't." Mom sat back up, and she was flipping through her folder. She held up the printout of a map and squinted at it. "Yes, we need to get back on Thirteenth Lake Road, see?" She held the map over to Dad, marking a place with her index finger. "This is Cemetery Road, where we are right now, see? And the lodge is here, on Thirteenth Lake. Stupid map isn't to scale, though."

"David, yeah, we need to get back on Thirteenth Lake," Dad said. "Follow me." He disconnected the call and dropped the phone back into the drink holder.

"You have arrived at destination," the GPS insisted again.

"Shut up," Dad said, shutting it off and smiling back at me as he shifted back into drive. The rain was still coming down pretty hard, a steady heavy drumming on the roof, and he made a three-point turn as I stared out the window. *Something seems familiar about this place*, I thought but dismissed it from my mind immediately. I'd never been to upstate New York before, so how could it look familiar?

But I couldn't shake the feeling.

I looked down Cemetery Road as Dad made the turn back onto Thirteenth Lake Road, and the feeling was gone almost as soon as it had come.

My phone vibrated again, and I pulled it out of my pocket. Mom and Dad were discussing the directions to the lodge and paying no attention to me.

We need to go ghost hunting later in the cemetery.

I grinned.

Carson Wolfe was a few months older than me. He'd always been my favorite—he could make me laugh really hard, and he always could come up with something for us all to do. I looked out the back window. The Wolfes had rented an enormous black luxury car, which made Mom roll her eyes and shake her head slightly. David Wolfe owned a television production company in Los Angeles, and Carson had become obsessed with the paranormal ever since his father started producing that crazy cable TV show about ghost hunters two years ago. We'd traipsed over Sanibel Island several times last summer looking for ghosts in cemeteries and trying to find haunted houses. I knew he'd spent most of this summer interning on the show—it was all he ever posted about on Facebook.

Well, that and links to articles about hauntings.

Carson had always had a kind of obsessive personality, even when he was younger. It seemed like every summer he was obsessed about something new—dinosaurs, European royalty, UFO's—and now it was the paranormal. He was a smart kid, one of those people who never forgot anything they read and could make straight As without studying that hard, a trait I envied. He'd been heavy when he was a kid, with strangely skinny arms and legs and a bit of a round torso. The Wolfes lived in Beverly Hills, and his parents had gotten him a personal trainer when he hit puberty—they always claimed it was because he was clumsy, to help him develop and improve his coordination. Mom, on the other hand, thought it was because they "couldn't have a fat son in Southern California." Carson wasn't overweight anymore—he'd developed some nice muscle tone and was always deeply tanned—but he was still clumsy. But not because he was uncoordinated—he was clumsy because he was always lost in thought and didn't pay as much attention as he should. Mrs. Wolfe bought him nice, expensive clothes, but Carson always seemed to put on clothes that didn't match because to him, a shirt was a shirt, even if it was orange and he was wearing green shorts.

I started to type a response when I noticed I had zero bars.

I sighed and put my phone back away. *I hope this is just a dead spot and my phone can get service at the lodge.*

I couldn't help but smile a little bit. No cell phone service, the place is on Lake Thirteen, and the GPS can't find it. This is like the start of one of those slasher movies, like *Friday the 13th*. That was about a camp up in the woods, too.

Marc loved slasher movies.

That was the real reason not having cell service was going to drive me crazy—not being able to text or talk to Marc whenever I wanted.

I missed him already so much I could scream.

It's only seven days and you'll be home next Sunday, I reminded myself as I looked out the window. We were still climbing, and the rain was still pouring down—I could hardly see anything outside. It was also getting later, and there hadn't been any thunder or lightning in a while.

I shivered again and closed my eyes, yawning.

I opened my eyes again when the car stopped.

There was another road branching off to the right, but we'd gotten much higher on the mountainside. I squinted to try to read the signposts.

"The sign says Thirteenth Lake Road goes off that way, but that's not what my map says." Mom's voice was annoyed, and I couldn't help but grin. She hated it when things didn't go the way they were supposed to. "The map says to keep heading straight up the side of the mountain, on the same road."

"Does the map name this side road?"

I closed my eyes and tuned them out.

I missed Marc.

I started to drift off to sleep, my parents' voices just noise, droning on in the background. I hadn't slept well last night, and Mom had gotten us up ridiculously early for the trip to the airport. I was sleepy, and so felt myself drifting off.

In the dream I was walking through the woods. The sun was shining and it was a warm spring day, and I was sweating just a little bit. But my heart was singing because I was in love and was going to be seeing my love in just a moment or two. A bee buzzed past my head as I walked, and I stopped to pick some beautiful yellow wildflowers growing in a bunch just to the side of the path. I held them up to my nose and took a deep inhale. It was a beautiful day, and it felt good to just be alive. I kept walking down the path and came around a corner. There, the path started sloping downward to a clearing where a log cabin sat. There was a well, with a brick wall built around it and a hood with a bucket hanging down from a crossbeam by a rope. There were rose bushes blooming in front of the cabin, and my heart leaped a bit in my chest. I saw Marc come out of the cabin door, wearing nothing more than a pair of old-fashioned trousers that looked strange on him, and he looked up to see me standing on the path, and his freckled face broke into a big smile, the sun glinting on his coppery red hair—

I was startled out of my nap by the sound of my mother swearing loudly.

"This stupid damned road just circled back to the original one!" I could tell by her tone she was getting angry, the way she always did when things didn't follow her plan. "Are we just supposed to drive around the side of the stupid damned mountain all night?"

"It's okay, honey," Dad answered, in the patented calm-Mom-down voice he'd perfected over the years, as I stretched in the back seat and looked out the window. "We'll get there."

The rain had stopped, but an eerie mist had come up. As I stared into the woods, the mist seemed to make shapes out in the forest, weirdly ghostlike, and I shivered. The dream had been so peculiar—it wasn't weird for me to dream about Marc the way I had, but what was weird was how I'd seen him in the dream. Those old-fashioned pants and the cabin in the clearing—what was that all about? It didn't make any sense, but then again, it was just a stupid dream. "Are we lost?" I asked, stifling another yawn.

"I think I've got it figured out," Dad said with a cheerful laugh, looking at me in the rearview mirror. "The directions and the maps were bad, is all. I think it should be right around this next curve."

I saw a wooden building out the side window, with a paved parking area in front of it. The porch light was on, shining yellow.

"That should be Iroquois Cabin," Dad said as the road climbed even more steeply. "And up ahead…"

We went around the curve, and there it was, with a big sign in the grass where the road widened into an enormous parking lot: MOHAWK LODGE AND RESORT. It was a long, two-story wooden building, and a yellow porch light was on by the front door. There were some other wooden buildings on the other side of the parking lot. Dad made a U-turn and parked, the headlights of the SUV shining in the wispy mist that seemed to be rising out of the grass. Another yellow light cast light on the other side of the big building, and through the mist I could see that the lawn sloped gradually downward to the silvery surface of a lake, glittering in the moonlight.

I shook my head. It all seemed so—so familiar somehow…but that had to be my imagination.

Dad shut the engine off, and the other two vehicles also parked. He grinned at Mom and winked at me. "All right, I guess we should get all checked in, don't you think?"

I opened the door and climbed out. The night air was heavy and damp enough to make me sweat, but it wasn't that hot. I yawned and stretched, and followed my parents inside. Just inside the front door there was a small gift shop off to the right, with a cash register on the counter. An enormous room stretched out in front of me. An area that looked like a dining room was separated off from the main room by a split-rail fence, and there were some tables on this side of the fence as well. In the dining room, the outside wall was lined with windows—but I couldn't really see anything other than mist through the glass. There were couches and rocking chairs spread out around an enormous fireplace, and stuffed animals lined the mantelpiece—I recognized a raccoon and an armadillo. Deer heads and some shiny fish were mounted on the dark paneled walls, glassy black eyes staring out over the room.

It kind of gave me the creeps.

A woman with long gray braids hanging from either side of her head came through swinging doors just past the fireplace that I assumed led to the kitchen. She was wearing a blue denim shirt, jeans, and a white apron. She was wiping her hands on the apron as she came toward us, a big smile on her face. "I was getting worried about you," she said when she reached us. "I'm Lisa Bartlett. Welcome to Mohawk Lodge and Resort."

"We'd have been here sooner but the directions—" Mom started to say, but Dad cut her off quickly.

"We're here now, that's all that matters." He held out his hand. "Hank Thompson. This is my wife, Arlene, and our son, Scotty."

"We're very delighted to have you here," Mrs. Bartlett said. Her smile hadn't wavered at all, even when Mom had started to get a little bitchy about the directions. "Let's get you all checked in. You're the only guests we have right now—summer is our slow season."

Dad and Mom followed her into the gift shop, and I wandered across the room to the split rails separating the dining area from the living room. I took the step down into the dining area and crossed over to the big plate-glass windows. I heard the front door open and close behind me as others in our little group came inside, and I could hear some talking but didn't pay attention to any of it as I stared down the long lawn to the surface of the lake—Lake Thirteen. Something was nagging at me, but I couldn't quite put my finger on what it was. Every time I thought I almost had a hold on whatever it was, it was gone. I sighed and pressed my forehead against the glass. There was a porch running along that side of the lodge, with a railing made of the same raw-looking split wood. I could see tables and chairs made from unfinished wood placed at even intervals along the porch, and there was a tire swing hanging from a pine tree just at the far edge of the lawn.

Everything seemed so familiar—like I'd been here before.

But that wasn't possible. I'd never been to Mohawk Lodge before.

It didn't make sense.

I shook my head and turned away from the window. I couldn't help but grin when I saw my mom hugging the Wolfes and the Starks.

Our fathers were pledge brothers at Beta Kappa fraternity at the University of Virginia. Our moms went there, too—that's where they all met. The three families took turns choosing the group vacation destination—last year had been our turn, and we'd chosen a beach house on Sanibel Island in Florida. We'd been taken a little aback when the Wolfes chose this place—they'd gone in the winter—but Mom and Dad were determined to make the best of it. I'd done some web searches—Mom's passion for American history was going to require visits to nearby Fort William Henry and Fort Ticonderoga. With Lake Thirteen right here, the Hudson River a short drive away, and all kinds of hiking and bike paths through the woods, there would be plenty to do during the day.

At least, that's what Mom kept saying, like she was trying to convince herself.

"I know it's silly," Mom had said one night over dinner, after the plans had been finalized, "but just the *name* makes me nervous. Lake Thirteen? It just seems unlucky, is all." She shivered as she passed me a bowl of garlic mashed potatoes. I tried to hide a smile without much luck, and she made a face at me. "Laugh at me all you want, mister," she wagged a finger at me. "But I've got a bad feeling about this trip. Mark my words, something bad is going to happen up there."

Dad and I had exchanged glances and tried not to laugh at her. Mom had never really gotten past her bad feeling, but you'd never guess it by looking at her hugging Aunt Lynda.

"Dude!" Carson Wolfe gave me high-five as I walked up. Carson was short, maybe five-six at most, with dirty-blond hair, a round face, and big blue eyes. He lowered his voice as he looked at me over the top of his glasses. "Ghost hunting later, right? You up for it?"

I tried not to smile. "Sure." I shrugged. "Why not? Where's Rachel?" Rachel was his sister. She was a year younger than us.

He rolled his eyes. "She wouldn't get out of the car." He started to say something else, but I was distracted by a big hug from his mother.

Lynda Wolfe was a small woman, barely five feet tall, and looked like she didn't weigh more than ninety pounds. Her thick black hair was parted in the center and pulled back into a long ponytail, the way it always was. Her skin was tanned, but her face looked different somehow in a way I couldn't quite identify. "You're such a big handsome young man now," she said in her breathless way, her smile widening as she looked up at me. I smiled as her husband crushed my right hand and yanked my arm up and down overenthusiastically. David Wolfe looked like he'd gained some weight in the year since I'd seen him last, and he barked questions at me without giving me a chance to answer.

That hadn't changed.

"Logan and Teresa are outside playing soccer," their mother, Nancy Stark, said as she kissed my cheek and gave me a hug. Nancy Stark was the tallest of the three adult women, almost my height, and also really thin. She smelled slightly of roses. She also had a dark tan, and her brown eyes were warm.

Her husband, Jerry, shook my hand less vigorously than Uncle David had and started quizzing me about my tennis game. "Maybe we'll have some time to hit the ball around some," he said as my dad came back out of the gift shop with the keys to Iroquois Cabin.

I excused myself as my father greeted his old friends—the usual shoulder punches and affection in the form of insults they never seemed to grow out of—and slipped back out the front door. Teresa Stark, wearing an orange Longhorn Football T-shirt over a pair of white shorts, grinned at me and jogged over to where I was standing on the cement sidewalk between the front door and the parking lot. Behind her, her twin brother Logan swore—he hadn't been able to stop the swing of his leg, and the ball went sailing down the sloping lawn past where Teresa had been standing. I willed myself not to watch him running and smiled as Teresa gave me a big hug.

Teresa was about five-eight and, like her mother, wore her brown hair cut short. She wore round gold-framed glasses on her pert little nose over her wide brown eyes. She smiled with her entire face, from her pointed chin to her round cheeks, her eyes crinkling in pleasure. She rarely wore makeup, and she wasn't wearing any at the moment. She had beautiful skin that always seemed to glow, and she was always tanned golden from playing soccer and softball. She was effortlessly good-looking and never really seemed to care how she looked.

Both Teresa and Logan were soccer stars at their suburban Dallas high school, with a strong chance of getting college scholarships to keep playing. But while Logan was lazy about studying, Teresa was a straight A student with her sights set clearly on law school.

"You look good," Teresa hugged me again. "It's so good to see you!"

"You, too." I replied, hugging her back. I still felt a little awkward around her, even though clearly the coming out e-mail wasn't a big deal to her. I hadn't thought it would be—Teresa had always hated injustice, which was why she wanted to be a civil rights attorney. That's part of the reason I was so surprised she never answered me. "What do you think of this place?" I gestured with my hand, and out of the corner of my eye I thought I saw something at the tree line on the other side of the parking lot.

I turned my head, but there was nothing there at all.

"Are you okay?" Teresa asked, her smile fading into a frown.

I turned back to her slowly. "You didn't see anything over there, did you?" I pointed, starting to feel more than a little foolish.

She shook her head. "No. No, I didn't." She peered at me over the top of her glasses. "You sure you're okay?"

As she said the words, once again I had that weird sense of familiarity—

And for just a moment, the pavement changed into dirt and rock—

And just as quickly changed back.

I gulped. *What the hell was that?*

"You look pale," Teresa reached over and felt my forehead with her right hand. "You're not hot." Her eyebrows knit together. "You sure you're feeling okay?"

"I didn't sleep good last night," I said, forcing a smile on my face. "I'm just really tired." *And I'm seeing things.* I stole another glance over to the edge of the forest. There was nothing there, nothing at all. *You're just tired,* I said to myself again.

"Okay," she nodded, leaning in closer to me as Logan approached, the soccer ball tucked under his arm and a big grin on his face. "We don't care about the gay thing, you know, you're still Scotty, if that's what you're worried about, okay? We wanted to talk to you in person—not online, okay?" Impulsively, she planted a kiss on my cheek.

I hadn't realized until that moment just how tense I'd been about it. I wiped at my eyes, turning my head slightly so she couldn't see the sudden tears her words had caused. "Thanks," I said softly as Logan slugged me in the arm.

"Come on, Scotty," my mother called. "Logan, Teresa—we'll see you at dinner."

"See you guys in a bit," I said, trying not to yawn, and I walked across the parking lot and climbed into the backseat of the SUV.

"Any trouble?" Mom asked as Dad started the engine.

"Nope," I replied, closing my eyes and leaning back into the seat.

But I deliberately avoided looking at that spot in the tree line as we drove past it.

I was just tired, that's all it was.

A short nap before dinner was all I needed, and I'd be fine.

CHAPTER TWO

All six of the adults were sitting in the lodge's little bar, drinking too much and laughing a little too loudly as they relived the glory days of past vacations and their college days— stories we'd all heard so many times before on the first nights of previous vacations I could probably recite them word for word. Once the reminiscing started after dinner, the five of us had gone into the game room. The game room was a small space through a door off the big main room. It had its own little bathroom and a back staircase leading up to the second floor. There was a desk with an ancient desktop computer sitting on it in one corner, and the wireless router was right behind it. There was a dusty air hockey table and a battered foosball table against the wall by the staircase. Right behind the L-shaped couch was a stack of well-worn board games, with Trivial Pursuit, Life, and Monopoly on the top. And in front of the couch was a coffee table, its top scattered with old issues of *People, Us Weekly, Better Homes and Gardens,* and *Good Housekeeping.* There was a big picture window with the curtains pulled open along the wall facing the lake, but it was now so dark outside the glass might as well have been painted black. An enormous flat-screen television was mounted on the wall opposite the couch and a cheap plywood entertainment center set beneath it, with stacks of DVDs and ancient videotapes on its shelves—mostly Disney movies and other so-called "family" entertainment. Of course, there was just basic cable.

And the game room of the lodge was the only place on the entire property with Internet access. The wireless signal was pathetic—none of us could get online anywhere else on the property. But no matter how many times we complained about it, that wouldn't change. And the zero-bars thing? Not just a dead spot—there was no cell service here, unless you drove down the mountain back to the state highway.

Mohawk Lodge and Resort was a bit on the rustic side, to say the least.

I was sitting at the round table off to the side of the room away from the window facing the lake, near the desk and the game tables. I frowned at my phone. Marc still hadn't answered my last text, nor had he sent me an e-mail. I scrolled through my Facebook news feed, but no one had posted anything new since the last time I'd checked it. I typed in *I am so bored I could scream* but deleted it without posting it. I put my phone down and leaned back in my chair, staring up at the ceiling.

I'd taken a nap after we'd gotten settled into Iroquois Cabin, which was just down the mountain road a bit from the lodge—Dad had been right about that. The Wolfes were staying in Algonquin Cabin, which was even farther down the mountain, and the Starks were in Huron—I wasn't quite sure where that was exactly. My room was huge, with its own bathroom and its own little back deck made of raw wood. I'd gotten a little creeped out when I checked it out—stepping out there, with its railing and three steps down to a dirt path that led back into the forest. It was the same feeling I'd had up in the parking lot at the lodge, like someone was watching me. But I knew that wasn't possible, so I went back inside, locked the door, and put the chain in place. I unpacked quickly and lay down on the bed, closing my eyes and falling asleep almost immediately.

We hadn't driven back up for dinner—Mom insisted we walk up the road. The path behind my room actually was a shortcut to the lodge but, "No taking the shortcut after dark," she'd warned me as we climbed up the steeply inclined road. "No telling what's out there in the woods."

I thought about pointing out that the *road* also went through the woods but bit my tongue. It was amazing how dark it was—I could barely see more than a few feet in front of me. Dad had brought a flashlight he'd found in the kitchen, and he kept it aimed on the road ahead of us. But soon enough we went around the curve and could see the yellow light on the side door, and Dad switched off his flashlight.

The Wolfes and Starks were already there, talking and laughing. Mr. Stark and Logan pushed two tables together, while a girl who introduced herself as Annie Bartlett offered us menus. She was a pretty girl about our age but seemed a little shy. She had light brown hair that reached her shoulders, freckles across her pert nose, and pale skin. She was slender and was wearing a pair of low-rise jeans underneath a red T-shirt with Mohawk Lodge and Resort written across the front in black letters. I saw Logan smirk on the other side of the table as she gave him a menu, and Teresa rolled her eyes at me. I knew that smirk—I'd seen it on Logan's face plenty of times before on previous trips.

Poor Annie was going to get the full blast of Logan's lady-killer charm.

After she took our orders and went back to the kitchen, he whispered to me, "Ten bucks I can get in her pants before we go home."

"Pig," Teresa said, punching him in the arm. "You leave that poor girl alone."

Logan winked at me when Teresa turned back to Rachel.

And after dinner, the adults went to the bar and we all came into the game room.

I picked up a worn deck of playing cards from the table and shuffled them, spreading them out into a game of Solitaire.

I wished someone would say something, anything, to break the horrible silence in the room. *We're all bored*, I thought as I placed a red nine on a black ten, *and that always winds up getting us all into trouble.*

Just the previous summer, on Sanibel Island, boredom was why we'd gone out in the boat moored to the house's dock without permission and wound up marooned on a deserted barrier island, requiring rescue from the Coast Guard.

Our parents hadn't exactly been thrilled about that one, to say the least.

I looked over at the brown couch, where Teresa was frowning in concentration at one end as she played Angry Birds on her iPad with the sound off, her tanned legs curled up underneath her. She looked up from the screen and caught me looking at her, responding with a big smile that lit up her face. She'd changed into a navy blue T-shirt and a pair of matching shorts.

Her right eye closed in a wink and her grin got wider.

"It's so damned boring here," Logan said, closing the cover on his own iPad and setting it down on the coffee table. He ran a hand through his already messy light brown hair. He blew out a breath and made a face at me, crossing his eyes, sticking out his tongue, then rolling his eyes. "Why the hell did they decide to come here in the summer? It's a *winter* place. And there's nothing for us to *do*." He started bouncing his legs rapidly. He'd never been able to just sit around—he'd always been a bundle of barely contained energy looking for an outlet. Even when he was a kid he'd never been able to sit still. The Starks had banned him from caffeine and sugar, but that hadn't helped much. That was why they'd put him into sports to begin with—to try to burn off some of that excess energy. It was the smartest thing they could have done. Logan loved playing sports, and he'd turned out to be a natural athlete—he had an uncanny command of his body and more than enough coordination to pretty much master any sport he tried.

If I was going to be completely honest, Logan was the one I'd worried about the most—he was such a straight-boy jock stereotype, always talking about all his girlfriends back home and flirting with every girl who got in range. If any of our little group was going to have a problem with me being gay, I'd figured it was most likely going to be him.

Like his twin, Logan had fair skin and light brown hair. Unlike Teresa, his hair was always out of control because he couldn't be bothered to concern himself with it. He combed it whenever he got out of the shower and never gave it another thought the rest of the time. He just didn't care. Logan was gorgeous and athletic—and girls *worshipped* him, if the comments and posts on his Facebook wall were any indication. All the years of playing sports and the weight training that went with it had given him the kind of body I would have gladly sold my soul to the devil to have. He was a couple of inches over six feet tall, with broad shoulders, a ridiculously narrow waist, and a defined stomach so flat and firm you could bounce quarters on it. His arms were thickly muscled, with veins bulging in his thick forearms and well-developed biceps. Years of running up and down a soccer field had given him strong, powerful legs and a round, hard butt. Like his twin, he didn't care too much about his clothes—he seemed to always be in soccer shorts and tank tops or sweats, and about half the time his clothes clashed. Unlike Teresa, he was rarely, if ever, serious about anything. He was a bit of a clown and could always make me laugh. His handsome face was strangely elastic, and he could twist it in the most ridiculous ways. He was always making jokes, and he couldn't stand just sitting around. He was up for anything, anytime—as long as it didn't involve just sitting.

He was also a really good guy with a big heart. Just before we sat down for dinner, he'd given me a big hug and whispered in my ear, "You can be as gay as you want, bro, but I hate to disappoint you, man—I'm just not interested." Then he laughed so loud everyone had turned to look, and I couldn't help but grin back at him.

He really was a great guy—but I still felt bad for Annie Bartlett. He was a heartbreaker.

"You guys want to go ghost hunting?" Carson Wolfe looked up from the book he was reading—*Ghosts of Louisiana: Stories of True Haunting*—dog-earing the page and closing it. He pushed his wire-framed glasses back up his stubby nose and grinned. "We could go see if that cemetery is haunted. I bet it is—the town dates back to colonial times. There's bound to be a ghost or two there, don't you think?"

"Shut up already," his younger sister Rachel said, almost absentmindedly. She didn't even look up from her own iPad, still launching birds across the screen without missing a beat as she spoke. "Besides, you don't know if there's a cemetery here. And even if there is one, I doubt the locals would like us messing around in there at night. In fact, I can guarantee they wouldn't—it's disrespectful." She waved a hand, still not looking up. Rachel was a pretty girl, with flawless white skin, bright blue eyes, and thick, dark curly hair. Like her brother, she'd been chubby when she was younger, and she'd had a rough time with acne for a few years. But she'd blossomed the year before the Sanibel trip. Now she had an amazing figure, with nice legs and curves that wouldn't quit. Last summer, Logan had made a couple of passes at her, but she'd shot him down cold. "Let's not forget the great boat-trip disaster of last summer." She looked up and made a face at her brother. "Besides, cemeteries are kind of creepy. Not to mention, you know, snakes and things." She gave a delicate, ladylike shudder. "No, thank you."

"Don't be like that, Rachel. If there's a Cemetery Road, there *has* to be a cemetery—they wouldn't call it that if there wasn't one," Carson insisted, his blue eyes wide open in excitement behind his thick glasses. "And I bet it's an old one! Come on, it'll be fun." He looked around at the rest of us. "What do you say, guys?"

"I'm in," Logan replied, standing up and stretching so that his T-shirt road up over his flat, defined stomach and the trail of light brown hairs leading down from his navel to the waistband of his shorts.

No surprise there, I thought, trying not to stare at his ripped abs. Logan's hands brushed against the low wood ceiling when he stretched. In his burnt-orange tank top and black nylon shorts, his legs bouncing in place, he seemed like an electrical wire wrapped up in a muscular teenager's body. "I'll see if Mom and Dad will let me take the SUV." He got up and bounded out of the room before anyone could stop him or say anything.

The Starks lived in Dallas, in a gated community in a rich suburb. Uncle Jerry was a heart surgeon, and Aunt Nancy was a perfect doctor's wife, a stay-at-home mom whose family was her number-one priority. She also did a lot of charity work for kids with cancer. The Wolfes, of course, lived in Beverly Hills ("9-0-2-1-0," as Rachel liked to say with a big bored eye roll), and Uncle

David owned a production company with several television shows currently on the air. The Wolfes weren't filthy rich, but they were pretty well-off. Aunt Lynda didn't work either—"She shops," I'd heard my mom once say dismissively when she didn't think I could hear her.

Yes, it's going to be a long boring week, I thought as Logan came bounding back into the room, brandishing the keys with a huge smile on his face. "Come on, let's go!"

"You can stay here if you want, Rachel," Carson said with a sly smile as he stood up. "You don't have to come with."

"Why not?" Rachel yawned and closed the cover of her iPad. "I'm sick of killing pigs. But I'm going to kill *you* if there are snakes."

I got up and stretched. I wasn't so sure this was a good idea, but figured how much trouble can we get into at a cemetery? Besides, my only other choice was to stay behind by myself and go listen to the boring college stories of the glory days at Beta Kappa.

Not much of a choice, really.

We trooped through the main room of the lodge. Our parents didn't even look up at us as we passed by, focused instead on their card game and the story my dad and Uncle David were taking turns telling, big stupid grins on their faces. It was a story I'd heard a million times before—the Great Panty Raid on Delta Zeta sorority, when Uncle David had broken his ankle and had to limp out of the house while the sorority sisters threw things at him. But when we reached the front door, my dad called after us, almost as an afterthought, "You kids be careful, you hear? Don't be getting into trouble."

"Sure thing, Dad," I said just before I went outside, waving back and smiling. The door shut behind me and I suppressed a shiver.

It was ridiculously still and quiet outside.

And it was *really* dark outside the cone of yellow light from the bare bulb next to the side door.

"They're okay with us going to the cemetery?" I asked as we trudged across the parking lot. I wrapped my arms around myself and didn't look over to the tree line. There was still mist, and it was cooler now than before, but there was still some damp to the air.

"I told them we were just going to drive down to the lake," Logan admitted. "They don't have to know exactly where we're going, do they?"

I bit my lower lip and hoped nothing went wrong.

There was no sound other than the occasional call of a bird piercing the stillness inside the woods. It was so dark I couldn't even see the lights Mom had left on at our cabin, even though I knew it was just through the forest. There was no one else staying at Mohawk—we had the place to ourselves, although the Bartletts, who owned and ran the place, said some townspeople might come up for dinner at the lodge restaurant every night. The moon came out from behind clouds and shone on the surface of the calm lake. A shiver went down my spine. It had been a lot warmer when we'd arrived, but it was still muggy and warm. The SUV chirped and its lights blinked as Logan clicked the doors unlocked.

Teresa hooked her arm through mine as we walked across the gravel parking lot. "You're awful quiet," she said, tilting her head so it rested against my upper arm as we walked. "Not like you. You haven't said much since we got here."

I shrugged.

"Is it the gay thing?" she lowered her voice. "Were you worried about how we'd react? Because you didn't have to be." She rubbed her hand on my back. "I told you, we're good. Logan will make some stupid jokes but they won't mean anything. We have some gay kids at our school and Logan's fine with it. He may not be the brightest but he's not mean." She shrugged. "As for Rachel and Carson, who knows? They live in Beverly Hills, so I'd imagine it's no big deal for them, either."

"Yeah, Logan said he was cool with it before dinner, and Carson seems to be pretty cool with everything." I said cautiously as we reached the SUV. "But Rachel hasn't said two words to me— not even hello."

Teresa shook her head as we got into the backseat of the SUV and mouthed the word *later* at me. I slid across the seat, and she climbed in next to me, shutting the door as Logan started the ignition. I was sitting in the middle, with Rachel on my other side.

She didn't look at me—she was fiddling with her phone, trying to get a signal. I leaned my head back and closed my eyes as Logan backed out of the parking spot.

The gay thing.

I swallowed and took a deep breath.

No one back home knew. But I hadn't wanted to spend another vacation lying to my oldest friends in the world. I'd *always* hated lying to them, pretending I had girlfriends who didn't really exist, joking with Carson and Logan about how hot some women were— last summer on Sanibel I'd hated being dragged along with Logan when he went on the prowl for some, as he called it, *summer lovin'*.

I hadn't told my friends at Farmington High School and wasn't sure if I wanted to, honestly. I hated lying to them and would decide to tell everyone—and then would completely lose my nerve when I was around them. Mom and Dad didn't even try to hide how relieved they were when I agreed to wait until college to come out. I didn't like the idea of lying to everyone at school for another year, but I could deal with it if it made my parents feel better. What was another year?

Besides, coming out at Farmington High really depended on what Marc wanted to do.

Marc.

Just thinking about Marc made me smile, the way it always did. Marc was the greatest, Marc was awesome, Marc was the sexiest hunk at school…but Marc also didn't want anyone to know he was gay.

The Kruegers lived a few houses down the street from us. Marc usually came over to my house, but every once in a while I had to go over to Marc's, and I never felt comfortable there. I never had, in all the years I'd known Marc. His dad was always home, it seemed, with a beer in his hand. Mr. Krueger didn't work—he'd gotten an enormous settlement from a work accident a few years before they'd moved to Farmington. Mrs. Krueger worked as the school secretary at the high school. Their television was always turned on to Fox News, and Mr. Krueger was always yelling about faggots and blacks and Mexicans and feminists and pretty much anything the television told him he was supposed to be angry about. One night when I was there and we were doing our geometry homework, he'd lurched into Marc's bedroom, going on a lengthy tirade about how the whole country was going to hell because of communists and socialists and Nazis and the coloreds and...

I'd felt sick to my stomach the rest of the night, only feeling better when Marc walked me to the front door when our homework was done and stole a quick kiss. I'd walked home on air.

I was lucky to have Marc, even if Marc wasn't ready to be as open as I wanted to be.

Marc is perfect, I reflected as Logan maneuvered the big car out of the parking lot and headed down the winding mountain road.

The Kruegers had moved down the street the summer before I started high school. Eighth grade had been rough for me—I'd started changing physically during the eighth grade, the pimples, my voice deepening, hair sprouting out where hair hadn't been before—and that was also when I'd started noticing things I hadn't noticed before. Things like my tennis coach's strongly muscled hairy legs, for one, or Tommy Gargaro's biceps and chest for another. The big family trip that summer had been to the Florida Gulf Coast, and I couldn't stop stealing glances at Logan's body on the beach, the way his skin turned golden brown from the sun, the golden hairs on his legs and forearms...I'd had some embarrassing dreams about Logan that trip, dreams where we ended up kissing on the beach and...

Those dreams hadn't stopped when the trip ended, either.

But as soon as I saw Marc, it was like Logan had never existed.

Marc was gorgeous. Logan was good looking, but Marc was maybe the best looking boy I'd ever seen in my life. If Logan was a nine, Marc was at least a twelve plus. Marc was better looking than most models and actors on television, and his body was just amazing.

The first time I saw Marc was when I walked down the street to get a look at the family moving in. There were some movers in coveralls unloading the truck, but just as I reached their property the front door opened and a boy my age came out of the house. I caught my breath and just stared as the boy came down the front steps and walked toward me.

Marc was taller than me—even now as almost-seniors Marc was a good two inches taller—and had thick blond hair the sun had bleached white on the top, but was darker underneath. He had wide blue eyes, thick red lips, and a strong chin. He wasn't wearing a shirt and had a strong muscular chest and a flat stomach. His arms were also muscular, and the jean shorts he was wearing fit snugly in the thighs. He was one of those lucky blonds who tan golden brown, and he was very deeply tanned. He held out his right hand. "Hey, I'm Marc."

"Scotty," I'd somehow managed to blurt out as we shook hands, wondering if Marc felt the same electric shock I had when our hands touched. "Welcome to the neighborhood...I live up the street a bit. Where'd you come from?" *Heaven?*

Marc had looked away. "We lived on the south side of the city." He looked back. "My dad had an accident at work, and he got a settlement." He seemed ashamed and anxious to change the subject, so we talked about school. Marc, it turned out, also played baseball, like me, but not tennis—he was a football player. It turned out we had a lot in common—comic books, the Hardy Boys, sports—and during our freshmen year we became best friends.

And I was crazy in love with Marc.

And we shared our first kiss last summer.

Everyone was thrown forward suddenly when Logan slammed on the brakes without warning.

"Jesus, Logan!" Teresa snapped. "Pay attention!"

"Sorry," Logan said as he shifted the vehicle into park. "I almost missed the turn. It just kind of snuck up on me."

The SUV had stopped just past the gravel road with Cemetery Road on the signpost. Logan shifted into reverse and backed up. We sat there for a moment, the headlights lighting up the woods on either side of the road.

I looked out the back window. The red glow of the taillights seemed to be swallowed up in the thick blackness.

"I wasn't even going that fast," Logan said defensively. He shifted the car back into drive and began slowly creeping along the road. "But this is Cemetery Road. Keep an eye out for the cemetery."

Nobody said anything as the car moved down the road, the only sounds Nicki Minaj on the stereo and the tires crunching the gravel. Teresa squeezed my leg, and when I looked at her, she smiled. I smiled back at her.

The car went around a curve in the road and there was an opening in the trees on the right, just ahead.

"Looks like we found it," Logan said as he slowed down even more.

There was an iron fence running alongside the road, maybe about six yards away, on the other side of a ditch. I turned my head and could see the entry road to the cemetery and a big gate. Logan carefully turned the SUV off the road, and in the headlights we could see, written in wrought-iron letters across the top of the big iron gate: NORTH HOLLOW CEMETERY.

The gates were open.

Shouldn't they be closed? A chill went down my spine. *Maybe we shouldn't go in here.*

I had a really bad feeling.

But I didn't say anything.

"Awesome!" Carson was practically bouncing up and down in his seat with excitement.

"Okay, here we go," Logan said and drove into the cemetery.

CHAPTER THREE

The car rolled to a stop about twenty yards inside the gate. Logan turned the engine off, and we sat there in a hushed silence.

The only sounds were the tick of the cooling engine and our breathing on the inside—and the windshield started fogging up.

I felt uncomfortable, like something was just not right. I shifted in my seat. I opened my mouth to suggest we leave but stopped myself. It was weird, but I felt anxious, like something was about to happen and the only way to keep it from happening was for us to back up and get the hell away from the North Hollow cemetery. As each second ticked past, the anxiety continued to grow stronger. I swallowed because my mouth and my throat were dry. Teresa gave me an odd look and handed me her bottle of water. I took a big drink and handed it back to her. She gave me a reassuring smile. She gently patted my leg. "It'll be okay," she mouthed at me.

I just smiled back at her and swallowed again, closing my eyes and trying to control my growing anxiety. I felt like I'd walked into a class to discover I'd forgotten we were having a midterm and hadn't studied at all. I shook my head slightly, trying to get a grip on myself. It's not like I'd never been to a cemetery before. Granted, this was the first time I'd ever been to one at night, but there were no such things as ghosts—no matter how badly Carson wanted to believe they existed. It was no different than being here during the day, I reminded myself.

But it was still pretty dark out there.

I shifted a bit in my seat again. I inhaled sharply. On my left, Rachel looked away from her phone long enough to give me a weird look, her eyebrows raised. She leaned in close to me and whispered, "Dad's TV show is a bunch of bullshit, you know, for idiots who *want* to believe in this kind of stupid shit." She rolled her eyes. "And Carson's the biggest idiot of them all." She looked back at her phone and grinned. "Oh my God!" She squealed loudly, holding the phone up so I could see it. "Look! *Bars!*"

"I knew I should have brought my phone," Logan said from the front seat. "Who knew the cemetery would be the only place up here you can get a signal?" He laughed. "All right, then." Logan turned to look at us in the backseat. "What's the plan, yo? We just gonna sit in the car all night, or are we going to find some ghosts?" He reached over and high-fived Carson.

"Let's go!" Carson said, his voice excited as he opened his door and the dome light came on. He slid down out of his seat and leaned back inside the car. He pushed his glasses up and waved at the backseat. "Come on, you guys, let's get a move on." Without another word he slammed his door shut and started walking down the dirt road. I could clearly see him in the headlights. Logan followed suit, slamming his door and hurrying to catch up to him. Rachel opened her door with a sigh and shoved her phone into her shorts pocket.

I closed my eyes and took a deep breath. The feeling was still there and was getting stronger. My stomach felt like it was knotting and my heart was beating fast. I felt like I might throw up. *This isn't right, this isn't right, this isn't right* kept running through my head.

"Aren't you coming?" Teresa asked, putting her hand on my shoulder. "Or are you just going to sit in the car? You know, that's not such a bad idea." She made a face. "There're probably mosquitoes and bugs everywhere around here. And snakes." She shuddered. "I *hate* snakes."

"I don't think snakes are nocturnal," I said, closing my eyes and taking a deep breath. I let it out. "All right, I'm coming." I undid the buckle of my seat belt.

But I didn't want to get out of the car.

I don't think I've ever been so afraid in my life.

I shook my head. "You're being an idiot," I said to myself under my breath. "What is there to be afraid of? It's all in your head." I forced a smile on my face for Teresa's benefit and slid across the seat. I stepped down out of the SUV, my feet sinking into the soft dirt on the side of the road.

And as soon as my feet touched the ground, the anxiety disappeared like it had never existed in the first place.

I actually felt a rush of joy so intense I couldn't stop myself from grinning from ear to ear and almost laughed out loud. I rose up on my toes and turned my head up to look at the stars blinking in the dark purple sky. I felt *alive,* like I could fly, so happy and free—

But just as quickly as it had come, the feeling drained out of me.

And I felt weirdly *empty.*

Weird, I thought to myself as I took a look around. I rubbed my bare arms. Goose bumps were rising on my skin, and I shivered a little bit.

The cemetery was longer than it was wide, stretching maybe thirty yards on either side of the dirt road in the center to where the tree line started again. I could barely make out the wooden fence in the darkness as I shut the door behind me. It looked to be, from the entry gate to where the gradually downward sloping cemetery ended at the fence and the forest, maybe two or three hundred yards long. It looked like there was a big drop-off just on the other side of the fence at the end because the headlights were shining into the tops of pine trees. The moon came out from behind some clouds, and I shivered again. The air was moist and sticky, but it felt colder than it had when we'd gotten into the car. There was a slight fog rising from the ground, and in the beam of the car's headlights I could see that some of the graves had small American flags planted on them, just in front of the headstones.

"I wonder what's the deal with the flags?" Teresa asked, wrapping her arms around herself, her voice hushed. "Look at them all. They look relatively new, don't they?"

"Doesn't the VFW put flags on the graves of vets on the Fourth of July or Memorial Day?" I whispered back to her, stepping off into the ankle-high grass alongside the road. The tall grass was a little damp, and I itched where it brushed against my legs. Teresa walked around to the front of the car, but I didn't go with her. The temperature was dropping, and dropping fast. I rubbed my arms just as more goose bumps came out of my skin—the hairs on my forearms were standing straight up. I rubbed my forearms, trying to get warmer, and my teeth started chattering.

Teresa and Rachel hurried to catch up to Logan and Carson, who were talking in hushed voices I could barely hear—all I heard was some mumbling. The cold was getting even more intense, which didn't make any sense. I blew into my hands, trying to get them warmer. All of the hair on my arms was now standing up, and when I put my hand on the back of my neck, my skin felt like ice. They'd probably make fun of me for not going with them, but I didn't want to—and I didn't care if they did tease me or call me a fraidy cat or something equally stupid.

I was starting to feel uncomfortable again, and when the moon went behind some clouds, it took all of my self-control to not open the car door and climb back inside.

I wished I'd grabbed a sweatshirt. I should have known the temperature would drop.

But what I really wanted was for us to just get back into the SUV and head back up to the lodge, where it was warm and—

Safe.

You're really losing your mind, aren't you? I chided myself. Like Rachel had said, it was just a graveyard, and there were no such things as ghosts. I took another deep, calming breath like Mom always told me to do whenever I was nervous and about to panic, and cleared my mind.

When I opened my eyes, I felt a lot better and started looking around. I was still cold, but it wasn't that bad.

The cemetery was unlike any other I'd ever seen before—not that I had a lot of experience with them. My dad was originally from rural Virginia, in the far western part of the state near the Kentucky state line, and whenever we went there to visit my paternal grandmother, we always made a pilgrimage to visit my grandfather's grave at

Four Corners Cemetery by the Baptist church. That cemetery was different than this one. At Four Corners, the graves were all lined up in neat rows so you could walk around without ever worrying about stepping on a grave by mistake. Here, the graves weren't placed in even rows—it didn't look like any thought had been put into placing them at all. They were scattered everywhere haphazardly, like when someone died they just picked an empty space regardless of where the other graves were placed. There was no rhyme or reason to it at all. In some places, the headstones were no more than a few feet away from the side of the road. The headstones themselves were an odd mix of shapes and sizes.

It felt like it was getting even colder, and the fog rising from the ground was getting thicker around my ankles, with little wisps floating up into the air and dissipating. I looked over at my friends. They'd stopped walking about twenty yards down the road and had gathered around a massive headstone about fifteen yards from the side of the road. I bit my lower lip. I wondered what they were doing and if I should join them, but somehow I couldn't make myself walk down there.

You're safer here—it's better not to go down there. Stay close to the car.

I shook my head. Maybe I *was* losing my mind.

I stepped back up out of the grass and leaned with my back against the SUV. There was a large old headstone not ten feet from where I was standing.

It won't hurt you to go take a look at it, now would it? What are you so afraid of, really? It's just a headstone.

I walked through the ankle-high grass until I was standing next to the headstone. It was remarkably large, so big it seemed like it should have more than one name carved it into, like a married couple's or maybe even an entire family's. The ones this size at Four Corners in Virginia usually did.

But the carving on the face of this one simply read:

ALBERT TYLER
June 10, 1890–August 20, 1907

"How sad," I said without thinking about it, "he was only seventeen." *And we have the same birthday.*

As I knelt next to the tombstone, an overwhelming sense of sadness swept over me.

It was so intense I felt tears swimming up in my eyes.

My heart was breaking, and I had to stifle a sob.

How awful to die so young, I thought, wiping at my eyes and looking over to the next headstone. It was slightly larger, and *Tyler* was also carved into it, close to the top. Underneath, there were two gray boxes with names carved inside. The one on the left said *Abram* with the dates March 7, 1858–September 12, 1920 underneath. The right read *Sarah,* and the dates of her life were April 2, 1866–January 3, 1965.

Another tear ran down the side of my face and I swiped at it. "You poor thing," I murmured. "You outlived your son by almost fifty-eight years. How *awful* for you that must have been. Did you ever get over it, Mrs. Tyler? Can you get over something like that?"

The sadness—the *sorrow*—swept over me again, and as my eyes filled with more tears, I couldn't help feeling a little confused. *Why do I feel so bad for these people I don't even know? What's wrong with me? Why is this affecting me so strongly?*

Almost the moment I thought that, I remembered the day when I was thirteen when Mom and Dad had to have my cocker spaniel, Skipper, put to sleep. I remembered my mother herding him into his kennel and my dad carrying it out to the car—they wouldn't let me go with, so I'd already had to say good-bye to him, he had cancer and it wasn't curable, and Mom had wiped her own tears away as I buried my face in his neck and cried, it wasn't fair, he was a good dog—

I caught my breath as I forced down a sob.

I hadn't thought about Skipper in years. Why now? Why here, of all places?

And Marc flashed into my head, saying good-bye to him last night, and the sad look on his face as we hugged at my front door, and how he'd said *I don't know, I'm just afraid I'll never see you again* before he walked down the driveway and down the street to his own house, and how weird that had been, but I'd felt sad, lonely, and empty. It had taken me a long time to fall asleep.

I shivered a little as the moon went behind a cloud again. My back now felt so cold it was like it had turned to ice, just like my arms and shoulders and the back of my neck, and I wished again I'd brought a sweatshirt with me.

I took another deep breath and touched the tombstone for a moment, tracing the name with my index finger.

"I wonder what you died from, Albert," I said out loud. Of course, in 1907 it could have been anything—the flu, measles—back then, any number of diseases that nowadays were just nuisances were often fatal—

What is wrong with me?

—and the sorrow, that overwhelming sadness, was growing stronger and seemed to be seeping into every corner of my consciousness. I shivered again.

Out of the corner of my eye I noticed that everyone else had gathered around yet another tombstone closer to where I was kneeling next to Albert's grave. Teresa was waving at me frantically, so with one last glance at Albert's headstone, I stood up and walked down the slight slope, carefully avoiding stepping on graves.

The sadness started fading away but I was still cold.

"What's—" I started to say, but Carson shushed me.

"Look at the flags," Carson whispered. He pointed.

I turned my head in the direction they were all staring. Illuminated inside the vast swath of light cast by the headlights of the car were several graves with small American flags planted on them, a few feet from their headstones. There were five or six graves in close proximity, and all the flags hung limply except for one that was waving wildly in a nonexistent breeze.

And it was directly in the center of the grouping of graves.

"That's not possible," I heard myself saying in a low voice. "How can the other flags not be moving?"

"There's not any wind," Rachel said, her voice shaking a little. "No wind at all."

"Do you believe now?" Carson whispered triumphantly. "How else could that flag be moving if a ghost wasn't trying to get our attention?"

We stood there in silence for a few moments that seemed like hours, watching the little flag waving. Finally, Carson pulled a recording device out of his shirt pocket. "Come on," he whispered and started walking toward the grave. Logan and Teresa followed, but Rachel and I hung back.

"Creepy, huh?" Rachel kept her voice low. "Do you think it's a ghost?"

"I thought you said there was no such thing," I whispered back to her, unable to take my eyes away from the waving flag. "But what other explanation can there be?" I shivered again.

"Well, it's certainly not the wind." She shook her head. "Carson's going to be impossible to live with now." She sounded annoyed, as though a ghost had started moving the flag specifically to irritate her.

I didn't answer her and turned back to look back toward Albert's grave.

I could feel the sadness creeping back into me again, growing stronger with each second until I felt like all I wanted to do was curl up into a ball and just sob.

"Are you okay?" I heard Rachel asking in a strange tone. Her voice sounded hollow and distant, like she was standing a good distance away rather than right next to me.

I didn't answer her. Instead, I started walking back to Albert's grave, and vaguely I was aware of her following me, the sound of her feet swishing through the damp grass.

I felt numb and forced myself to swallow. The cold was getting more intense the closer I got to Albert's grave.

Isn't cold a sign of a haunting, didn't you read that in a book somewhere, that ghosts always bring cold with them?

I shook my head. *There's no such thing as ghosts. It's just getting colder out here, that's all.*

But the sadness—why was I feeling so sad?

I closed my eyes—

—and almost jumped out of my skin when Rachel grabbed my arm. "Come on," she whispered urgently, "let's go see what they're doing."

I opened my eyes and looked longingly back at Albert Tyler's headstone before reluctantly following Rachel away.

It didn't feel right walking away from Albert's grave.

But that didn't make any sense.

I looked back over my shoulder as we walked to where the others were standing. There wasn't anything there but a tombstone—but the sadness kept fading the farther I got from Albert's grave.

I turned my head back around when I heard Carson whispering urgently.

"Spirit, whoever you are, don't be afraid of us. We aren't here to harm you in any way. We're here to help you cross from this plane to the next. Don't you want our help?"

Out of the corner of my eye, I saw Rachel make a face and shake her head. Logan was trying really hard not to smile, but I could see it on his face, the way the corners of his mouth were twitching. Teresa's arms were crossed in front of her, and she looked bored, like she'd had enough and was ready to go.

My teeth started chattering from the cold, and I took a few steps back and away from Rachel. *It's amazing how fast it can get cold here in the mountains,* I thought again, rubbing my arms to try to get blood flowing through them and warm up. It bothered me they weren't taking Carson's ghost hunting seriously. Carson obviously believed, so the mocking was kind of mean.

They probably mock me behind my back.

I shivered again.

"Can you communicate with us? Can you say something, so we know you're there?"

The flag was still waving.

"Sometimes they speak in a tone we can't hear," Carson said softly. "That's why I have this digital recorder—it can pick up tones humans can't hear."

I opened my mouth to say something, but before I could get the words out, Carson, Teresa, and Logan all whipped their heads around in the direction of the end of the road, where the graveyard ended in a fog-wreathed fence.

"What was that?" Logan asked, his eyes round.

"I didn't hear anything," I said, and Rachel nodded agreement. "What was it?"

"I heard someone—or something—growling," Teresa said. "You didn't hear it?"

"I didn't hear anything," Rachel said.

"I heard it too—a growling, and it sounded like it was coming from over there," Carson said decisively. "By the fence, right? Come on, let's go see what it was."

He started walking quickly down the dirt road, with Logan and Teresa right behind him.

"No, thanks," Rachel said with a slight shudder. "I didn't hear it, and even if I did, something growling?" She winked at me. "It's probably just a dog or something, you know, no matter how bad Carson wants it to be a ghost."

"Yeah." I smiled back at her. "But, you have to admit, the flag is weird." I pointed to it.

And as soon as I did, it stopped moving.

"*That's* weird." Rachel frowned, moving closer to me. "I wish they'd come back so we could get out of here."

The other three were no longer in the light cast by the headlights of the SUV, but it looked like they were using the faint glow of their cell phones to see.

"I don't like cemeteries," Rachel went on. "This isn't a place where people are supposed to be, you know, after dark." She shrugged off her light sweatshirt and tied it around her waist.

"Aren't you cold?" I asked, surprised.

"Cold?" She gave me a funny look. "What do you mean, cold? I'm sweating. It's so muggy up here."

I closed my eyes for a moment and said, "Feel my back."

Rachel reached over and placed her hand flat against my back. Her eyes widened. "Your back *is* cold." She breathed out, pulling her hand away. "I—I don't understand. How is that possible?"

I bit my lower lip. "It's not cold out?"

"Scotty, it's warm and muggy." She grabbed my hand with both of hers, and I could feel how warm they were. "Are you feeling all right?" She put a hand to my forehead. "You're cold as ice!"

I looked back over my shoulder at the headstone. "I feel fine, I'm just a little cold."

It wasn't true, though—I still felt that weird, overwhelming sense of sadness. I walked away from Rachel and knelt next to the headstone yet again.

"How did you die, Albert?" I whispered as the sadness overwhelmed me yet again, my eyes filling with tears that I quickly wiped away before she could see them.

"Scotty?" Rachel said from behind me, placing her hand on my shoulder. "Are you okay?"

"I'm fine," I said, wishing she would just go away and leave me alone. I wanted to ask her to leave, to walk away, but I knew she would think it was weird, and that would make her only want to stay there all the more.

She'd always been my favorite when we were younger, and when she'd morphed from the girl with the braids who hung on my every word and whose face always lit up with joy whenever she saw me to the bored teenaged girl fascinated by makeup, clothes, and the latest teen idol, I'd been more than a little sad. Every summer I hoped she'd be excited to see me, the way she'd been when we were younger, but this year, like the past four or five, she'd just nodded at me after my parents hugged her and went back to playing with her phone, twirling a lock of her hair around her index finger.

So, of course, now that I wanted to be left alone, she couldn't catch a clue.

I heard her gasp. "He was so young!"

Go away, I thought, closing my eyes and willing her to go join the others.

I sensed her kneel down beside me. "Oh my God, he has the same birthday as you...he was the same age as you." She inhaled sharply. "That's just *weird.*"

I resisted the urge to tell her to go away, to leave me alone the way she had for the last five years. *We aren't friends anymore, you've made that clear,* I wanted to say, but somehow I couldn't bring myself to say the words.

The cold got worse on my back, it was like—it was almost like someone had opened a freezer door directly behind me, and all that foggy cold air was brushing against my back. All the hair on my arms and the back of my neck stood up again—I could see the goose bumps rising on my forearms, and the back of my head was cold.

"Oh my God, look at your arms." Rachel grabbed hold of my left arm, and her hand felt warm and damp on my skin. "Goose bumps! And you're freezing!" There was a catch in her voice I recognized as fear. I turned my head to look at her, and in the faint light where we were kneeling, I could see her face had drained of color.

She's really afraid, I thought in wonder, *so why aren't I?*

The only thing I'd felt was the sadness, and I realized as the cold on my back was getting more intense that the sadness was starting to fade away…it was still there, I was aware of it, but there was something more there…

But I couldn't experience whatever it was as long as she was there.

I had to make her leave.

And as soon as I thought it, a sound from the far end of the cemetery startled us both.

Rachel stood up. "I better go see what they're doing. If Carson kills himself I'll get the blame." She smiled hesitantly down at me. "Maybe you should go wait for us in the car."

"I'll be fine." *Just go already!* I stood up to reassure her, and she looked up into my eyes quizzically, touching my arms again.

"It's so weird, how cold your arms are." She shook her head again, like she was trying to figure it out for a moment before giving it up.

I watched her go, and the sadness began to turn to elation.

Yes! I exulted, joy and excitement rushing through me quickly, electricity that made the tips of my fingers and toes tingle—

—and just as quickly, it was gone.

The others were coming back up the road now, talking excitedly amongst themselves in low voices. Carson grinned. "You should have come down with us, bud! It was exciting!" He pushed his glasses back up his nose as he reached out and grabbed my arms. "Rachel said you had an experience up here, though." Carson's eyes narrowed, and he tilted his head sideways as he peered at me. "Your arms are cold…" He looked down at the headstone. "Interesting. Do you still feel the cold?"

"Not as much," I admitted, and it was true. It was like that freezer door behind me had been closed.

And as soon as that thought crossed my mind, I felt it again—a horribly sad coldness spreading from the back of my head down my back to my legs, and all of my arm hair stood up.

"Wow." Carson goggled at me, fumbling in his pocket for his phone. He touched my back and his eyes widened. "You're really cold."

But before he could take a picture of my arms with his phone, it was gone.

"Can we just get out of here?" Rachel whined. "I'm scared and don't want to be here anymore, okay? This place is creeping me out."

"Yeah," Teresa chimed in. "We can talk about it more up at the lodge—and listen to your recordings, Carson."

"Okay"—he nodded—"but first I need to say a prayer. Everyone close your eyes."

I closed mine, and after a few moments, Carson started speaking in a low voice. "Spirits of the cemetery, we thank you for the welcome and apologize for disturbing your rest. We are going to leave now and would like to remind you that no matter how much you want to come with us, this is where you belong now, and you cannot come back with us. Please, continue to rest in peace, and may God bless you all. Amen."

Everyone muttered *amen*, and we walked back to the SUV in silence.

As I opened the back door, I looked back over my shoulder at Albert's headstone.

Good-bye, I thought sadly as I climbed into the backseat.

CHAPTER FOUR

No one spoke as Logan started the SUV, and Nicki Minaj started rapping loudly through the speakers again. Carson leaned over and turned the volume down; maybe it seemed as inappropriate to him as it did to me.

I buckled my seat belt as he put the car into reverse and started backing out of the cemetery. Just like on the way down, I was sitting in between Rachel and Teresa. Neither spoke. Teresa just stared out the window, but Rachel took my hand in hers and squeezed. Her small, warm hand was trembling just a little bit, and I wondered what had made her so upset. I looked at her, and she gave me a strange looking smile that didn't quite make it to her eyes.

I looked away from her, past Teresa and out the window, as the SUV slowly backed out of the cemetery.

I don't want to leave. I want to stay here and find out—

Find out what? I wondered, even though the thought was gone almost as quickly as it had come to me. But I didn't want to leave with them. I had an urge to crawl over Teresa, open the door, and leap out. I wasn't supposed to leave, I was supposed to stay behind in the cemetery…

Rachel squeezed my hand really hard, and her well-manicured nails dug into my palm. I winced and pulled my hand away.

"Sorry," she whispered, but she still had that weird look on her face. With her other hand she smacked Logan's headrest. "Will you hurry up and get us the hell out of here?" she snapped.

"Chill, all right? I can hardly see anything behind us and I don't want to drive into a ditch," he snapped back at her. "Anytime you think you can drive better—"

"Just get us out of here," Teresa said, still looking out her window. "The sooner the better."

What's gotten into everyone? I looked over at Teresa. Her face looked pale in the dim light inside the car, and even Logan frowned in concentration as he stared out the back windows. Finally, he started turning the wheel as he backed out onto the pavement of Cemetery Road. A huge cloud of dust, churned up by the tires, followed us out as he shifted into drive and headed for Thirteenth Lake Road.

The weird feeling that I didn't want to leave, that I wasn't supposed to, that I should somehow stay behind got stronger as Logan drove slowly along the winding road. It was surreal, this sense that something was off and wrong, all the while Nicki Minaj kept rapping through the speakers. I felt a lump in my throat and tears coming to my eyes again, like I was going to start sobbing uncontrollably at any moment. I knew it was crazy, not normal, irrational—but I couldn't seem to control my emotions.

I felt like I was saying good-bye to Marc last night all over again, that he was walking down my front steps and down the driveway and I was never going to see him again.

But that doesn't make sense. I'm only going to be here for a week, we're flying home next Sunday and I'll see him that night, he's already said he'd come over and we're going to order pizza...

But I couldn't shake the feeling.

We came around a curve in the road and the headlights shone on the stop sign and the trees on the other side of Thirteenth Lake Road.

I closed my eyes and tilted my head back. *Think about something happy, forget this sad stuff, you don't want to start bawling your stupid head off in front of everyone.* Something happy. Like—how it was about a year ago that Marc first kissed me.

Just the thought made me smile.

Our first kiss had happened last summer, right after we got back from the Sanibel Island trip.

By then I'd long given up on anything developing between the two of us. No matter how much I wished and hoped and prayed for it to happen, no matter how badly I wanted Marc to be gay—it just wasn't in the cards. He was a straight boy, and that was the end of that. Other guys I talked with on the gay teen message boards kept warning me to forget about him—but that was easy for them to say. How could I forget about him when I saw him every day, spent every possible second of every day with him? Every night when I got in my bed and under the covers, the last thing I did before drifting off to sleep was replay the day. What did he mean when he said this? What did he mean when he said that? Reliving moments when our bodies brushed against each other, or when our arms bumped together, the way his muscles felt, how firm yet strangely soft his skin was. Glimpses of his body when he'd yawn and his shirt would ride up, or changing in the locker room for gym class, or the way his butt moved in his tight jeans as he walked away from me in the hall at school.

Yeah, the kids from other parts of the country I'd met online were probably right—we were never going to be together, and I was coming to terms with that—but I could dream about him all I wanted to, couldn't I? I could imagine what it would feel like to have his arms around me and his lips pressed up against mine all I wanted to, but that wasn't going to make it happen. No matter how much alike we were, no matter how much we made each other laugh, even though we finished each other's sentences and then would laugh till we cried and our sides hurt, it just wasn't meant to be. It broke my heart to see him going steady with girls, even though we never ever talked about girls when we were alone. I hated every one of his girlfriends, smiling and being friendly and polite while I really wanted to stab them all in the heart, shove them in front of a moving car, *anything* to get rid of them.

And I hated myself for feeling that way. I just couldn't stand anyone who would take him away from me.

And, last summer, I'd finally accepted it, once and for all.

Marc had gotten a job as a lifeguard at the town pool. He didn't want to work at the pool, he'd explained to me after he got the job.

His dad was making him work for the summer "to teach him the meaning of hard work and the value of a dollar." I resisted the urge to point out that his rotten father hadn't worked since they'd moved to Farmington—Marc knew it as well as I did, after all, and what good would it do to point out that his dad was a big loser?

It was going to be the worst, most boring summer of my life.

The one good thing was he'd broken up with his latest girlfriend—that empty-headed cheerleader Tori Crawford—on the last day of school, so she was out of the picture. I'd tried really hard to like Tori, but she made it impossible. She was one of those girls whose whole life revolved around their boyfriend, and she always spoke in some kind of baby talk to him that was supposed to be cute but was really just annoying. I didn't understand what he saw in her, but she was pretty enough and had a nice enough body, if you were into girls. So at least I didn't have to worry about sharing his free time with her.

But the summer turned out to be even worse than I could have dreamed. He had to be at work every day from ten in the morning until the pool closed at eight. By the time he punched the time clock and walked the two miles home, he was exhausted and just wanted to go to bed. He was off on Wednesdays and Sundays, but his dad kept him busy doing yard work and chores around their house. Every time I saw him, he was so tired and worn out he could barely speak in anything more than words of one syllable and grunts.

I tried hanging out at the pool, and managed to get really tanned, but it was so *boring*. He had to sit in his lifeguard tower, so high up we had to shout at each other to be heard. We could talk when he had his lunch break, but that was about it. And all the little kids running and yelling and splashing while their mothers talked to each other and ignored them drove me crazy. I read a lot of books while my skin got darker, headphones firmly in place trying to drown out the screaming of the kids—how Marc stood all the noise was beyond me—and tried to sneak glances at him, up on the tower behind his dark sunglasses, as his skin turned golden and the sun bleached out the hair on his legs.

And that had to be enough for me. To see the sun glinting on his muscles as I watched the girls in their bikinis flirting with him, my heart aching as I rode my bike home when I couldn't stand to be out in the sun anymore, hoping that he wouldn't be too tired to stop by and hang out for a while.

He rarely wasn't, as June turned into July, and next thing I knew it was August and time for the annual family vacation.

Pretty much our only contact all summer long had been through text messages and posts on Facebook.

It was the worst summer of my life, and I couldn't wait for it to be over. At least when we were in school, we saw each other all the time—we were both in the college-prep program and always took as many classes together as we could manage.

I didn't even get to see him before we left for Sanibel. He was supposed to come over the night before we left, but he texted me that, once again, he was too tired—and he'd see me when I got back. *I miss you so much,* I typed out…but deleted it instead of sending it.

We're not even friends anymore, I thought, burying my face in my pillows, not bothering to respond to his text. The job was worse than any girlfriend. Feeling like an idiot for crying over someone who didn't feel the same way about me that I felt about him, I vowed to myself that when I got back from Sanibel I was moving on.

I'd find a boyfriend if it killed me.

But the night we got back from Sanibel, I was in my room unpacking. I'd gone completely incommunicado there—I didn't even take my phone with me on the trip, so I avoided Facebook and e-mails and everything. I figured it was better not to be tempted to send him desperate texts, to pour all my feelings for him out in an e-mail, or whatever. I was miserable, of course, the whole time we were in Florida, but nobody seemed to notice because I'd gotten really good at pretending to be happy when I was miserable—just like I'd gotten really good at pretending to not be gay, or pretending Marc was just my best friend. On the flight back to Chicago, I decided I was tired of pretending. About everything.

It was on the plane I decided I was going to tell my parents I was gay. I was going to tell everyone, and I didn't care if it cost me friends or if kids picked on me at school or said nasty things to me on Facebook or Twitter. No matter how bad it got, it couldn't be any worse than lying to everyone, including myself.

I was putting my duffel bag away in my closet when I heard knuckles rapping on my doorframe. "Come in!" I'd called without turning around, figuring it was one of my parents.

"Did you have fun in Florida?"

I spun around. Marc was standing in my doorway, and my heart melted at the sight of him. He was wearing a white ribbed tank top with the big red cross on the front with *Lifeguard* written underneath in red block letters and his loose red board shorts. His hair was almost white from sun bleaching, and his skin was the darkest reddish-gold I'd ever seen. There were places on his shoulders where the skin was flaking away, the aftermath of a burn. He was looking down at the floor.

All my good intentions about putting distance between us went right out of my head at the sight of him. I loved him even more than I had before I'd left, if that was even possible. "Yeah," I mumbled uncomfortably. "You?"

"You never answered any of my texts or called me back." He moved into the room, still not looking up from the floor

His voice sounded so despondent, miserable, and sad I wanted to just put my arms around him and hold him, comfort him.

"I didn't take my phone with me," I replied, amazed my voice wasn't shaky. "I forgot it and didn't even realize it until we were halfway there." So much for being honest with everyone—I hadn't even been home for an hour and I was already lying again.

"You could have e-mailed me and let me know."

I didn't know what to say to that, so I didn't say anything.

"Are you mad at me?" This time he looked up, and his beautiful blue eyes were swimming in tears. "What did I do, Scotty? Whatever it is, I'm sorry."

"You didn't do anything." I stepped past him and closed my door. I could hear Mom and Dad talking in the kitchen. *I have to tell him the truth, even if it means he turns away from me in disgust.* I bit my lip. "Sit down." He sat on the edge of my bed and stared at the floor. I sat down in my desk chair. "It's not you, it's me." I swallowed, searching for the right words to say, and finally decided to just say it. "I—I don't think I can be friends with you anymore, Marc. It's too hard for me."

He looked at me, and the naked pain in his face broke my heart into about a million pieces, but I couldn't worry about his feelings anymore. I had to do what was best for me.

The words started coming out of me in a rush.

"I'm gay, Marc, and always have been and I'm in love with you but I know you're not in love with me you're not gay but it's hard you're my best friend and I don't want to put you in an awkward place and it's so hard to be so close to you and not be able to tell you how I feel and I've missed you so much this summer and—"

He stopped me by leaning forward and putting his hand over my mouth. He licked his lips. "You're in love with me?"

I nodded.

His face lit up with a huge smile, the one that always made my knees weak. "But Scotty, I love you, too." A tear dropped out of his right eye. "I didn't think…I never dreamed—"

I didn't let him finish. I leaned over and kissed him.

And it was better than I ever had imagined it could be.

"Looks like no one's here." Logan's voice cut into my reverie, startling me back into the present as he pulled into a parking spot at the lodge. "I guess they went back to the cabins." He didn't shut the car off, but turned around and looked at us in the backseat. "Maybe I should just drop everyone off. What do you guys want to do?" He frowned. "I can't believe they just bailed on us like that."

Carson opened his door. "You can drop us off later." He got out of the car and stood there impatiently, tapping his foot in the gravel. "We need to write down our impressions of what happened at the graveyard while it's still fresh in our minds and listen to the recording to see if any ghosts tried to communicate with us." When no one responded or moved, he grew more impatient. "Come on, you guys. I know you don't take any of this seriously, okay, but I do." His voice took on a whiny pleading note. "Come on, you all heard that growling sound. And what about what happened with Scotty? You think that was nothing?"

Rachel blew out her breath and opened her door. "We might as well humor him, guys," she said, sliding down to the ground, "or we'll never hear the end of it." She gave me another weird look and shut the door.

What's wrong with her? I wondered, sliding across the seat to follow Teresa out the other side. Logan shut off the engine and turned off the lights. Now the only light was the naked bulb by the screen door leading into the lodge.

The air was thick, warm and heavy, almost syrupy. Beads of sweat popped out on my arms as I walked across the parking lot to the sidewalk to the entryway. *It is humid and muggy,* I thought as I opened the screen door and went inside. *So what was all that cold down at the graveyard?*

The big front room of the lodge seemed much creepier when empty than it had earlier. It was a long room, with couches and chairs scattered around a massive fireplace. The animal heads stuffed and mounted on the rough-hewn walls had seemed almost funny in their tackiness in the daylight, but with all the windows big squares of darkness, they seemed scarier and more menacing. I swallowed and sat down on one of the couches in front of the fireplace. Rachel plopped down next to me and patted my shoulder. She just smiled when I looked over at her. "How do you feel?" she asked me in a low voice.

"Fine," I replied. *What the hell is she talking about?*

"Anyone want a soda?" Logan asked as he walked over to the big red Coke cooler in the far corner of the room. He lifted the lid and some fog escaped. He came back to where we were sitting, passing out Cokes and Diet Cokes.

I popped the top of mine and took a long drink, smothering a belch as Carson started passing around our iPads. "I can't believe they went back to the cabins and just left our iPads lying around in the game room," he said with a scowl.

Logan rolled his eyes as he flipped open the case to his. "It was probably our parents' idea." He mimicked his mother's voice. "If someone steals their iPads it will teach them a lesson about running off and leaving them out."

"Yeah, yeah, sounds like my mom, too." Carson rolled his eyes as he sat down in a wooden rocking chair and opened the cover of his iPad. "Everyone write down your impressions of the graveyard and what you saw," he ordered. "Everything, no matter how unimportant it may have seemed, because you never know—coupled with something someone else saw, it could be something important." He looked around at all of us. "Please take this seriously, guys."

Teresa winked at me as she sat in a chair beside him, and I hid a grin. I sat down and opened the Notes app and started typing with two fingers, feeling kind of crazy and stupid.

Away from the cemetery, in the big well-lit room with the staring bears and wolf heads on the walls, I didn't really know what to type. In the cemetery, the coldness, the sadness and the weird flag thing had seemed like proof there was such a thing as ghosts. Now, it seemed unreal, like all of our imaginations had been working overtime or something down there. But I started writing because I knew Carson was going to want us to compare notes when we were all finished.

But I didn't mention Albert's grave as I touched the letters on the screen.

That seemed *private* to me, like it wasn't any of their business.

It didn't even seem weird that I felt that way.

So I just wrote about the weird solitary flag waving, and the weird sensation of cold on my back and my arms. I didn't mention the sadness—I was the only person who'd felt that.

I had just finished when Rachel sighed. "Okay, finished. What do we do now, Scooby-Doo?"

Carson gave her a dirty look. "You know, I don't make fun of your bullshit interests, do I?"

"All right, I'm sorry." She stuck her tongue out at him.

"Is everyone finished?" Carson asked. When everyone nodded, he had us each read out loud what we'd written down.

I went first, rushing through it as quickly as I could and putting my iPad down. I didn't listen to any of the others, letting my mind wander back to saying good-bye to Marc last night.

Marc hadn't gotten a job as a lifeguard this summer—we'd both gotten jobs working as stock boys at the Jewel-Osco. We'd even convinced the manager to let us work the same shifts, so I could give Marc rides to and from work, since he didn't have a car and Mom let me take hers. It was perfect. The job itself was meaningless—all we had to do was restock the store and make sure everything was nice and neat and organized looking. It paid much better than lifeguarding, and we got to spend almost all of our time together.

It had been the opposite of last summer. This one had been almost too perfect to be true.

"I wish you weren't going away," Marc said as we lay side by side on my bed. "And I'm sorry we can't...you know." He was always apologetic about his fear of coming out, like I somehow didn't understand why he felt that way. All it took was listening to his father rant just once about the *goddamned homosexuals* for me to know Marc was much worse off than I was. No, I knew too well Marc wasn't ever going to be able to do anything about coming out until he was no longer under his father's roof.

We hadn't really thought that far ahead, of course, but I just figured we'd go off to college together, maybe share an apartment. I was looking at the University of Illinois—I really wanted to go to Northwestern, but it was too expensive, and there was no way I was going to get a scholarship. My grades were good but they weren't *that* good.

"It's only for a week," I replied, trying to be brave. He squeezed my hand so hard I almost cried out.

"It'll seem like forever," he replied gloomily. "You better answer my texts this year."

"I will," I'd replied, not knowing then there'd be no cell service and limited Wi-Fi on the mountain. I squeezed his hand back and lifted it to my mouth and kissed it. "You know I'll be thinking of you every second I'm there, and missing you so bad I won't be hardly able to stand it."

I'd walked him home—we'd kissed good-bye in the privacy of my bedroom—and he'd looked back to where I stood on the sidewalk one last time before he went into the house.

It felt like my heart was being ripped out of my chest.

"Interesting," Carson was saying as I focused on the present again. "No one else experienced the cold the way Scotty did—and neither Scotty nor Rachel heard the growling sound the rest of us did."

"What do you think it means?" Teresa asked. She looked interested, as did Logan, while Rachel looked like she wanted to start playing with her phone again.

"It means there was a dog or something—maybe a wolf—in the woods," Rachel said with a big yawn before Carson could say anything. "And it took off while you were on your way down to the fence. As for the cold?" She shrugged. "That I can't explain. But it was really weird, I'll say that, especially the way Scotty kept getting the goose bumps." She started playing with her iPad again, and I could see the Rio version of Angry Birds loading on the screen. "That was pretty freaky."

"You didn't feel anything but the cold, Scotty?" All of them except Rachel were looking at me now, expectation on their faces.

Tell them, what can it hurt? I took a deep breath. "I just felt really sad." I shrugged. "I don't know what else to tell you. I felt really sad." I swallowed. "I felt like I was going to cry, honestly. Now, it just seems weird. I don't know."

"And that's all?" Teresa's eyebrows came together. She was watching me closely, and I realized Rachel was, too. It was odd.

"Like I said, I felt like I was going to start crying." I shook my head. "I can't explain it any better than that—I'm sorry if it doesn't make any more sense to you than it does to me. I just felt really sad. I even started remembering my dog Skipper, you know, the day we had him put to sleep. It was like every sad memory I ever had came back to me, and that made it even worse."

"Ghosts—and hauntings—usually have the cold associated with them," Carson said, more like he was just thinking out loud. "Haunted houses have cold spots in them, and people who see or experience ghosts always say it got colder right before...but it was just your back?"

I nodded.

"There was a case"—Carson burst out—"I remember reading about it—sometimes ghosts hug you from behind, and you go back…I swear to God, I remember reading something like that earlier this summer, but I can't remember where."

He went on, but I wasn't listening anymore. I closed my eyes.

A ghost had hugged me? From behind? And then just held on to me?

I really didn't like the sound of that—but I couldn't help but wonder if it was Albert.

Carson got his recording device out and turned the volume all the way up before hitting play.

There was nothing but the sound of us walking around and whispering.

And then I heard it clearly—the growling sound. It was faint, like it was far away from where Carson was talking softly.

Carson switched the recorder off quickly. "Did you hear that?"

Even Rachel had looked up from her iPad. "That didn't sound like either a dog or a wolf," she said slowly, her face draining of color.

"It was human," Logan said, swallowing. "Play it again, Carson."

Carson fiddled with it for a moment, and then I could hear the growling again.

Rachel was right. It didn't sound like an animal.

"Who the hell was that?" Teresa whispered.

The recording kept playing, now with the sounds of the three of them whispering to each other as they ran down the road to the fence.

"There's nothing here," Logan said clearly on the recording.

"We should have brought flashlights. If we come down here again, we will," Carson answered him.

The quality of the recording was remarkable—not like every other time I'd heard a recording from a handheld before, where the voices sounded hollow and tinny. We heard them talk some more, and then, not hearing the growling or any other sounds, they headed back up to where Rachel and I had been standing.

"He's cold, feel his back." Carson's voice.

And then, clearly, we heard another voice say, *"Scotty."*

"Oh. My. God." Carson dropped the recorder. "Did you hear that? It said Scotty's name."

We all stared at each other.

"Who said that?" Teresa stared at me. "That didn't sound like any of us."

"None of us said his name, I'd swear to it," Logan replied, his voice shaky.

"Get real, it had to be one of us." Rachel reached down and picked up the recorder. She fiddled with it for a moment and hit play again.

"He's cold, feel his back."

And the voice said my name again.

It wasn't any of us.

I closed my eyes and remembered the sadness, the way the cold had started on the back of my head and traveled down my back, the way the hairs on my arms had stood up.

It was Albert.

Who else could it have been?

CHAPTER FIVE

Since our cabin was the closest to the lodge, they dropped me off first.

Both Rachel and Teresa hugged me before I went inside, Rachel holding on a little longer than was necessary. "Are you sure you're okay?" she whispered as she let go and stepped back away from me, her big blue eyes round and staring at mine.

"Yeah, I'm good," I replied, trying to laugh off how uncomfortable she was making me feel. "Really. I'll see you guys in the morning."

I waved after I unlocked the door to the cabin, and Logan turned the SUV around and drove out onto the road. I shut the door behind me and locked it. The door to my parents' room was closed, but I could still hear my dad snoring anyway. I smiled.

The cabin had a big living room with a little kitchenette tucked away in a corner, with two bedrooms on either side. My parents had taken the large bedroom on the right. The place was decorated in what my mother had rather snottily described as "early American lumberjack" when we'd arrived—the cushions on the big couch and the chairs were in a matching red, black, and white flannel, and over the fireplace a deer's head was mounted, and its big glassy black eyes seemed to always be looking right at me wherever I stood in the room. There was dark shag carpeting, and the walls were paneled in a faux-wood style that seemed right out of reruns of *The Brady Bunch*. I opened the door to the bedroom on the left and flicked the switch that turned on my bedside lamp before turning off the lights in the living room.

I shut my door behind me and leaned back against it. I was still a little spooked by everything—hearing that voice on the recording saying my name was probably the creepiest thing I'd ever heard in my life. I still wasn't completely convinced it wasn't some kind of trick Carson was playing on me, but that didn't explain the cold or the weird emotions I experienced in the cemetery. The bedroom was really cold, but that was because when we'd arrived it had been warm and stuffy and I'd turned the air conditioning unit in one of the windows on high. I turned it down, shivering, and stared out into the pitch-blackness of the night for a moment before reaching up and pulling the blinds down.

I spun around and dashed from window to window, pulling down the blinds and pulling the curtains closed. There was something frightening about the darkness, almost threatening…

And I laughed at myself. *It's just the dark, you idiot,* I reminded myself. *Are you afraid of the dark now like a little baby?*

There was a door on the back side of the room that led to a small patio deck. I made sure it was locked and the deadbolt slid into place, then sat down on my bed and took off my shoes and socks. Self-mocking aside, I still felt nervous and uncomfortable.

There's something out there that wants me and is dangerous.

I shook my head and took a deep breath as I slipped my T-shirt over my head and shivered again. It was still so cold in my room, even though the air conditioner was off. I looked over at one of the windows, thinking maybe I should open one, let some warm air in.

But I couldn't bring myself to get up and open the window.

I shrugged off my shorts and pulled back the covers, sliding underneath. *There's enough covers so I don't need to open a window,* I decided as I reached for the lamp on the bedside table. I turned it off and my room plunged into darkness. I closed my eyes.

The bed wasn't comfortable, and the pillows were flatter than what I was used to. I stared up at the ceiling for I don't know how long before I finally was able to drift off into a restless sleep.

And of course, I had a horrible nightmare.

I was in bed, but the room was different. My eyes were open and it was bright, moonlight was shining in through the windows, so I could see the cabin I was in was nothing more than just a big room, really. There was a rough-hewn door that closed and bolted, but the windows were open, and I could see the trees and the night sky. I was underneath a beautiful red and green quilt, but even though I was warm underneath the quilt I could see my breath, and it seemed like the air was getting colder with every breath I was taking. When I'd opened my eyes I had felt safe and warm, but not anymore— there was danger, I was in danger, something was coming for me, I needed to get out of the bed and get away from there, but I couldn't, I was frozen in place, and I could hear it, outside of the cabin, it was coming for me and it wanted me, it was evil and dangerous and was going to kill me—

I sat up in my bed, my heart pounding, gasping for breath in the darkness.

I tried to control my breathing, to get my heart rate to slow down, and I wrapped my arms around myself. It was still chilly in the room, but it was more stuffy than anything else, the air hanging heavy and damp. According to the glowing red numbers on the digital clock on the night stand, it was just after three in the morning. As my eyes adjusted, I could tell it was lighter in my room than it had been when I'd gone to sleep.

Thirsty, I slid out of bed and went into the little bathroom. I turned on the light and stared at my reflection in the mirror. My face was pale, and my eyes were red and bloodshot and swollen. I got a glass of cold water and gulped it down. I put the glass back on the sink and splashed cold water on my face.

"It was just a dream, that's all, and is it any wonder you had a nightmare after hanging out in a cemetery all night?" I said to myself in the mirror.

And that's when I heard it.

At first, I wasn't sure I was even hearing anything at all. The wind was blowing around the cabin, and I'd heard the trees in the forest just a few short yards behind the cabin rustling around ever since I'd woken up. Goose bumps came up on my arms, though, when I realized that the wind was trying to form words.

You're really losing it.

And then I heard it as plainly as I'd heard my name on Carson's recorder.

"Berrrrrrrrrrrrrrrrrrrrrrrrrrr-tiiiiiiiiiiiiieeeeeeeeeeeee."

Bertie.

Albert?

I sat down hard on the toilet and tried to stop trembling.

This was more terrifying than the dream or anything that happened in the cemetery.

You're still asleep that's it you're still having the dream focus and wake up, Scotty, before you—

And then I heard it again, the voice, calling.

It sounded so sad, heartbroken and lonely. It was hollow—it sounded like what the wind would sound like if it could speak.

"Berrrrrrrrrrrrrrrrrrrrrrrrrrr-tiiiiiiiiiiiiieeeeeeeeeeeee."

There was so much anguish in the voice, like whoever was calling Bertie was in great pain.

I stood up and walked to the back door. I felt like I had to, I didn't have a choice—the voice was someone suffering, someone is terrible pain, and I had to go outside and help.

I felt along the wall for the light switch I'd noticed earlier and flipped it up.

I turned the doorknob and stepped out onto the deck.

There was a light just outside the door, and the yellowish glow lit up the rough-hewn, unpainted deck and the three steps down to the uneven back lawn. The light faded just beyond the tree line, and within a matter of seconds some bugs and moths were flying around the light. I squinted, but I couldn't see anything out there. There was nothing to see, and no one.

The air was damp and there was a slight chill to it, but it was warmer out on the deck than it was in my room. It was still so incredibly dark outside—I could barely see anything outside the circle cast by the porch light.

I could see the path that led from the back steps into the woods fairly clearly. I'd noticed it earlier, when I'd checked out the patio after unpacking my suitcases.

"Berrrrrrrrrrrrrrrrrrrrrrrrrrr-tiiiiiiiiiiiiiieeeeeeeeeeeee."

The voice was heartbreaking.

I walked across the wooden deck to the stairs and rubbed my arms to warm them up. My skin felt moist and damp.

It was amazing how silent the night was, other than the wind, and how dark the woods were.

Surely there were some nocturnal animals? Where were the owls?

"Berrrrrrrrrrrrrrrrrrrrrrrrrrr-tiiiiiiiiiiiiiieeeeeeeeeeeee."

The sadness I felt earlier in the evening came back, filling me up like water being poured into a glass.

I felt like I was going to start crying.

I walked down the three wooden steps to the cold, damp grass. I felt like I had to find the person who was calling, take him in my arms and hold him, comfort and kiss him until his pain went away. I wanted to make his suffering stop.

I needed to make his suffering stop.

I started walking up the path, listening for his voice to come again. I stopped once I reached the tree line, peering through the darkness. I could vaguely make out the path as it wound deeper into the woods, beyond the warm yellow glow coming from the porch light. My own shadow stretched out into the woods before being swallowed by the darkness. I stepped into the woods—

—and froze in place.

The feeling of sadness and longing was fading rapidly, pouring out of me almost as quickly as it had poured into me. The wind was beginning to pick up, the trees and bushes rustling anxiously.

I could feel the temperature start dropping again rapidly. I started to shiver, my teeth chattering, and I could see my breath.

That's not possible.

I could sense it. There was something—something *else* out there in the woods, something other than whoever it had been calling, something dangerous and evil.

I started backing up, one foot behind the other, stepping back away from the woods and whatever was out there, my heart starting to pound faster and my breath coming in gulping gasps. I desperately wanted to turn and run, to get away from the dark and into the full safety of the light, back up onto the deck and slam the bedroom door behind me, turning the lock and sliding the deadbolt into place, pushing furniture over to block the door as an extra precaution, waking up my parents—

And tell them what, exactly? There's a ghost or something in the forest that wants to get you? Get a grip, Scotty!

But crazy as it seemed, I knew, could sense, that whatever it was, it wanted me.

I could hear it coming, the unmistakable sound of something moving through the underbrush—the sound of branches being pushed apart and bushes being moved aside as whatever it was headed directly for me, and just like the dream I'd had, I was rooted to the spot, unable to move, just stuck there, every nerve and instinct in my body screaming at me to move, run, get the hell out of there, and the terror just rose inside of me, taking me over completely—

—and I sat up in my bed again.

It was almost seven in the morning, according to the clock, and was already light outside. I could see gray light around the blinds on the window with the air conditioning unit—that weird mix of gray and light and dark.

As I sat there, yawning, I heard it again.

"Berrrrrrrrrrrrrrrrrrrrrrrrrrrr-tiiiiiiiiiiiiiiiieeeeeeeeeeeee."

And then, as it faded away, the goose bumps back up on my arms again, I began to hear the normal sounds of the woods—birds chirping and cicadas humming and insects buzzing. A car drove past on the road, heading in the direction of the lodge.

Everything was normal again.

Had it all just been a crazy dream?

I swung my legs to the floor and noticed that my feet were dirty.

I threw back the covers. There were pine needles and dirty leaves in my bed.

I started trembling as I got to my feet and walked over to the back door.

The deadbolt wasn't turned.

I swallowed.

It hadn't been a dream. I'd gone outside, into the woods, during the night.

Maybe I'd been sleepwalking. So my mind imagined everything because I was really asleep, but I was just awake enough to be aware of what I was doing?

I slid the deadbolt into place and walked into the bathroom. I turned the shower on and brushed my teeth. The face that stared back at me out of the mirror looked tired, scared, and not really myself. "There's no such things as ghosts," I told my reflection firmly.

I stood in the shower for a long time, letting the hot water soak into my body, soaping up and rinsing off, hoping the hot water would leech the cold out of my bones and my muscles. The shower seemed to be returning everything back to normal. By the time I turned the water off and reached for a towel, I'd pretty much convinced myself the entire thing had been a figment of my imagination, a combination of the power of suggestion from Carson's insistent belief in the paranormal, being physically tired from traveling all day, and emotional exhaustion from missing Marc.

After drying off and getting dressed, I went out the back door to the path. It was so strange how normal everything seemed. I could see my footprints in the dewy grass and, farther past that, my bare footprints in the dirt of the path—but they stopped halfway to the tree line.

"So I was sleepwalking and dreaming the rest," I said under my own breath, relieved there was a normal explanation for it, after all.

Still, as far as I knew, I'd never walked in my sleep before, but that didn't mean I never had. And both dreams had been so vivid—

—and don't forget what happened in the graveyard—

—and I'd heard the voice calling Bertie *after* I'd woken up.

But that was probably just a remnant from the dream, after all. The dream had been so deep and intense, I could easily have still been dreaming even as I was waking up. That made a lot more sense than it being something paranormal.

And of course, I'd heard *Bertie* because my subconscious remembered Albert's grave.

I went back inside and closed the door behind me. The room was getting stuffy again, so I turned the air conditioner back on, and I could hear someone moving around out in the living room. I opened my door and walked out there. Mom was in the little kitchenette, spooning coffee into a filter. She was wearing gray shorts and an orange Virginia sweatshirt, her hair was tousled, and she yawned as she put the filter into the coffeemaker and turned it on. "Morning." She smiled at me, fighting another yawn. "You're up early."

"I had trouble sleeping," I said as the coffee started brewing. My stomach growled.

"Did you kids have fun down at the lake last night?" she asked, giving me a tired smile as she sat down at the small round dining table. She yawned again. "I felt bad about not waiting up at the lodge until you kids got back, but we were all tired…and as your dad has to keep reminding me, you're not a child anymore. You're practically all grown up."

"Yeah, well." I felt myself blushing. "It was fine down there, I guess. We just hung out and talked, mostly. I couldn't believe how late we were down there." *If you only knew, Mom.*

"It's weird, I had trouble sleeping, too." She rubbed at her eyes. "As tired as I was, I thought for sure I'd sleep like the dead. It's the weirdest thing, you know—your dad snores, and I can sleep through that. I guess maybe I'm used to it. The Bartletts must have a dog or a cat, I guess. I'll have to ask them about that." She yawned again. "And ask them not to call it all night long."

I was reaching for one of the coffee cups in the cabinet over the sink when she said that, and I froze. "You heard someone calling?"

"Yeah." She smiled at me. "Pour me a cup, will you?" She shook her head as I passed her a steaming mug of coffee. "I mean, really. I get it, you know—if your pet gets out you want to find it and get it inside. I wouldn't want mine out all night with all the predators in the woods." She took a swig of her coffee and sighed in relief. "I sure hope they found Bertie."

My hand trembled as I filled a cup for myself. "Bertie?"

She nodded. "Was that what was keeping you from sleeping?" She went on as I sat down across the table from her, trying to keep my face expressionless. "I'm going to have to say something to Mrs. Bartlett about it today. I mean, they need to be a little bit more respectful of their guests' sleep, don't you think?" She winked at me. "I mean, we're not paying them a small fortune to stay here so we can't sleep at night."

"Yeah," I replied stupidly. I couldn't think of anything else to say.

She'd heard the voice, too. It wasn't a dream, it wasn't my imagination—someone had been out in the woods.

But it made more sense that it was one of the Bartletts out looking for a cat or a dog. I'd just heard the voice and worked it into my dream. And this morning, when I woke up, my subconscious mind had played a trick on me—I'd still been dreaming.

I wasn't going crazy.

"Did you hear it this morning?" I took another drink and kept my voice steady. The coffee was bitter and strong. I generally took creamer and sweetener in mine, but we didn't have any in the cabin—a previous guest had left the coffee behind.

"This morning?" She gave me a weird look. "No, I didn't. I told you, it was the middle of the night." She ran a hand through her curly brown hair, which she always kept cut short. "Did you? Surely they'd found whatever it was by then…Do you mean to say they were out there calling all night long?"

"It was probably my imagination," I said hurriedly. "I mean, I thought I did, but I was probably still half-asleep."

"So, how are the kids treating you?" She reached over and placed her hand on top of mine. I resisted the impulse to pull away—that would make her feel bad. "They're not…there's nothing I need to talk to anyone's parents about?" Her eyes took on a steely glint.

"No different, like nothing's changed." I shrugged. "It really hasn't come up much—just a couple of times, really, and when it does, you know, it's cool. They seem really happy for me." I rolled my eyes. "No big."

"You were worried, weren't you?" She gave me a sharp look. "I know I was. We thought about, you know, canceling the trip, but"—she sighed—"but we can't protect you forever, and there are people out there who are assholes about gays, you know, like that awful so-called church in Kansas." She made a face like she'd eaten something sour. "But much as I want to, I can't protect you from all the ugliness in the world." She got up and refilled her cup.

We'd had this conversation I don't know how many times since I'd told her and Dad. I got it, and I also knew how lucky I was. It seemed like there were always stories on the news about gay kids being bullied to the point they'd kill themselves, and my parents wanted to make sure that things never got that bad with me. So they were always checking on me and making sure I was okay—I'm almost certain they were monitoring my Facebook page and my Twitter—but there was no reason. I also knew if I ever told my parents people were bullying me—well, heaven help the bullies.

"Mom, you don't have anything to worry about." I rolled my eyes. "I'm fine, and everyone else is, too. It's just not a big deal. Yeah, I was kind of worried before we got here, but I should have known better, you know? They're like family. I just"—I bit my lip—"I just miss Marc. And I hate that I can't get a signal on my phone up here. I promised I'd call him and I can't unless I go into town."

"I know." She patted my hand. "I wish he'd been able to come with us."

"What?" I stared at her. "What do you mean?"

"Your dad and I thought it would be a nice surprise for you, you know, and have Marc come on the trip with us." She made another face. "I even went over to the Kruegers' house to talk to his parents about it. The way they reacted, you'd have thought I said I wanted to sacrifice him to the devil or something."

"You talked to his parents about him coming with us." I couldn't wrap my mind around it. They really were awesome parents—but Marc's…

"We even offered to pay his way, you know." She shook her head. "I thought his father was going to bodily throw me out of the house! You weren't kidding about his temper. I just apologized and got out as fast as I could. I won't make that mistake again." She blew out a raspberry. "I have to say, I worry about him and his sister with that man in the house with them. Just goes to show, you never know. I always thought he was a nice man."

"Yeah." Mr. Krueger was *always* on his best behavior when other parents were around—you know, adults who might call social services on him. It was creepy how good he was at acting like a great guy, which was completely different than how he was alone with his family. He could be ranting and raving the usual way, spittle flying from his lips with every word, and the moment another adult came around he changed, turned into a completely different person, laughing and joking, smiling and friendly. I never had gone into detail about how prejudiced he was to my parents—I just told them he drank too much and had a temper. I'm sure they thought I exaggerated. Parents never believe what kids tell them about other parents. "You didn't tell them about me and Marc, did you?"

"I promised you I wouldn't, didn't I?" She sounded exasperated. "It's Marc's business and Marc's decision when he wants to tell his parents. I don't think it's right, I don't think you boys should be sneaking around and lying to them, but after that meeting…I still don't think it's good to keep it from him, but I certainly can understand why he's reluctant. If that was my dad, I wouldn't tell him *anything*." She drummed her fingertips on the table. "Poor, poor Marc."

I'd worried all summer Mom would say something to the Kruegers. She just couldn't wrap her mind around the idea that any parent would throw their child out of the house for any reason—no matter how many stories she'd read about just that. She'd been terribly uncomfortable about Marc and me seeing each other without his parents knowing and hadn't agreed to it until Marc broke down and cried in front of her.

She still blamed herself for making him cry—which, I am not ashamed to say, I sometimes worked to my advantage.

"I can see on your face you're terrified I said something I shouldn't have," she observed. "Don't worry, I'm not stupid. All

I told his parents was your father and I thought it would be nice if you had a friend up here to hang out and do things with—but it's probably for the best, anyway. I wouldn't have been able to enjoy myself if I had to keep monitoring the two of you to make sure you weren't—"

"Mom!"

"I was a teenager once, too, you know." She went on like I hadn't said anything. "I remember what it's like. I just want you to be careful—and there's no need to rush, you know, you're still both teenagers—"

"*Mom!*" I knew my face was flushing furiously, and I was completely mortified. "So, what's the plan for today?"

"All right, all right." She held up her hands. "Excuse me for caring and worrying about my only child. I always forget that makes me a bad person."

"Mom—"

"Well, after breakfast we're all going down to the town to do some grocery shopping." She made a face at her coffee cup. "This coffee's just not going to cut it, and it seems silly to pay for meals when we have kitchens in our cabins, and that wonderful barbecue pit. You kids are welcome to come with—I think the men are going to see about making plans to go white-water rafting and find out about tours of Fort Ticonderoga and other places of interest around here. I don't imagine we'll be going anywhere other than down to town and back up here—there's plenty to keep us occupied around here for the day, don't you think?" She smiled. "I can see by your face you kids aren't coming down to North Hollow with us."

"We didn't really talk about it last night." I replied. We hadn't.

"Well, why don't you head up to the lodge and get some breakfast?" They served a buffet breakfast every morning in the dining room—it was included in the price of the cabin rentals. "I'll start the long process of getting your father out of bed."

Impulsively I kissed the top of her head, and she smiled.

I ducked back into my room to get my cell phone. I checked it; I'd plugged it into its charger when we'd arrived, and since I didn't have any bars I'd left it in my room all night. I started to grab my iPad, but decided against taking it. I could always come back for it if I wanted it.

I slid my phone into my shorts pocket and went out the front door of the cabin.

But instead of walking down to the road, I walked around to the back.

Mrs. Bartlett had explained to us that the path into the woods behind our cabin was an actual shortcut to the lodge—when you reached the fork you took the left one and it would lead you out to the parking lot eventually. She didn't say where the other trail led to, but since the place was primarily a winter sports resort, I assumed it was probably a cross-country skiing trail or something.

I walked up the path and into the woods.

It seemed perfectly normal, just a wooded mountainside in upstate New York. I saw some butterflies seem to float by. Somewhere in the distance I could hear running water. Birds were chirping and squawking as they flew overhead. It was getting warmer as the sun climbed higher in the sky, and through the branches I could see a perfectly blue sky, no clouds anywhere.

There was nothing scary or creepy about the path at all.

After about twenty yards the path veered off to the right, and then came around a corner where it forked in two directions. There was a weathered wooden sign with the word *lodge* carved into it, pointing off to the left. There was no sign for the other direction, and it seemed to slope downward while the one to the lodge sloped up.

I hesitated there. Obviously, the other path led deeper into the woods, but if there was a path, there had to be a *reason* for the path to exist. And surely if it was a cross-country trail, there would be a sign, right?

Something was pulling me in that direction, something inside me telling me to turn right instead of left.

But then my stomach growled and I remembered how hungry I was. I started walking toward the lodge.

I only looked back twice.

CHAPTER SIX

I was on my second plate of food when everyone else showed up.

By the time I came out of the woods at the lodge parking lot, my stomach was growling pretty constantly. I was so hungry I almost felt nauseous. The sun was shining, and at the foot of the long sloping lawn in front of the lodge, Lake Thirteen glittered silver in the bright sunlight. I pulled the door open and walked back inside the lodge's main room. At the far end, silver heating dishes with cans of Sterno burning underneath were set up, with two enormous industrial style coffee makers—the kind with a black spout you flipped upward to fill your cup. I could smell bacon and sausage and eggs, and my stomach growled even more. I got a cup of coffee and loaded up a plate with sausage and bacon and toast. I stepped down into the dining room and sat at a table next to a window, facing the front door. I scarfed the food down as quickly as I could, and had just sat down with my second plate—this time with a stack of pancakes and more bacon—when the front door opened and both the Stark and Wolfe families came in. I waved as they all made a beeline for the buffet table. I kept eating as the adults sat at a table on the other side of the room, and the kids plopped down at mine. Logan had more food on his plate than I'd had in both helpings. He grunted something I assumed was supposed to be *good morning* and immediately started shoveling food into his mouth.

"Revolting, isn't he?" Teresa said, taking the seat next to him and making a face. "Imagine having to look at that across the table every morning and every night. And if I'm not quick, he'll eat everything in sight and I'll starve."

Logan smiled at him briefly as he chewed, and flipped her off good-naturedly before going back to shoveling food into his mouth.

"How'd you sleep?" Rachel asked as she unfolded her napkin. All she had on her plate were a couple of pieces of buttered toast. She started spreading strawberry jam on one.

"Not good," I replied, pushing my plate away. I looked over at the table where the adults were sitting—my parents had also arrived, but their table was far enough away that I didn't have to worry about them overhearing anything we were saying.

"Nightmares?" Carson poured some cream into his coffee and stirred it.

I nodded and bit my lower lip. "Yeah. They were pretty awful. And I heard someone calling in the woods last night—calling Bertie. I thought it was maybe all a part of the dream, you know, but then this morning my mom said she heard it."

Logan started making *Twilight Zone* noises until Teresa smacked his arm hard.

I couldn't help but grin. In the well-lit dining room, with the sun streaming in through the windows and all the voices talking—it all seemed so unreal now. "Mom figured it was one of the Bartletts, looking for a cat or a dog or something." I shrugged. "But I don't know. It was the middle of the night when I first heard it—at least if I wasn't dreaming—and I heard it again when I woke up."

"They don't have any pets." Logan rolled up a piece of sausage in a pancake and poured syrup over it. "I talked to Annie yesterday—"

"Trying to get in her pants," Teresa interjected, earning a sour look from Logan.

"—and they don't have any. She had a dog but wolves got it last winter, and she said she doesn't want to get another."

"Interesting." Carson tapped his plate with his fork. "So, what did Scotty and his mom hear last night?" His grin was so smug I wanted to pop his balloon.

"Are you *sure* you weren't dreaming?" Rachel had finished her two pieces of toast and was fiddling with her phone again.

"It couldn't have been a dream—like I said, my mom heard it, too."

Carson looked like a cat who'd swallowed several canaries. "I told you it was ghosts," he said officiously. He looked over at the table where our parents were talking and laughing. "You're sure the voice was calling *Bertie*? That's what it was saying?"

I nodded.

He slipped his recorder out of his pocket and waved it at all of us. "Listen to this." He hit the play button. He'd cued the recording to just before we heard the voice say my name.

But it didn't sound like my name this time.

"I could have sworn it said Scotty last night," Teresa frowned.

Carson nodded. "Exactly. We weren't expecting to hear *anything,* and so when we did, our minds interpreted what we heard as something we were familiar with—we heard Scotty's name. After all, we were all keyed up from what happened down there—and what Scotty had experienced. So when we heard the voice on the recording, we heard Scotty's name. That's why it's so important to listen again when things have calmed down and—"

"It's saying Bertie," Rachel cut him off. "Albert, right?"

"That's what I heard," Logan popped the last of his weird pancake-sausage burrito into his mouth.

"So, once the adults head into town"—Carson glanced over at their table—"we should head into the woods and look around."

"Why?" Rachel looked up from her phone.

"Because that's where Scotty and his mom heard someone calling Bertie last night," he said patiently, like he was explaining to a small child. "Whatever the ghost wants us to know, I think we're going to find in the woods."

I pushed my chair back. "I'll be on the deck in a few." I took my plate and my coffee cup over to the buffet table, where a big gray plastic tub had been set out for dirty dishes. Mrs. Bartlett was standing there, wiping her hands on a dish towel. I smiled at her and headed to the game room, sitting down on the brown couch and pulling my own phone out of my pocket. I pulled up Marc's contact page and stared at his smiling face for a moment before texting: *Very limited access up here...no bars and having to use wifi to send messages...and limited wifi at that. I miss you.*

I sighed and erased the last three words. We always had to be careful with texts and e-mails—Marc's dad checked Marc's phone pretty regularly, and we couldn't take the chance that Marc would be able to delete things before Mr. Krueger got his hands on the phone. I hit send and closed my eyes briefly, then got up and headed out to the deck.

I heard voices from around the corner of the lodge, and a few moments later there was the sound of two cars starting. I turned my head and saw two cars head down the hill—all of our mothers in one, our dads in the other. I slid my phone back into my pocket just as the door opened behind me.

"I still think this is a really stupid idea," Rachel whined, folding her arms and sitting down on the raw wood railing. "Why mess with this kind of stuff? It never ends well in movies."

"No one's making you go with us," Carson retorted, his face reddening a bit. "And this isn't a movie, is it?"

She made a sour face. "Smart ass," she replied, leaning back against the railing. "Just because this isn't a movie doesn't mean this isn't a stupid idea." She turned to Logan and Teresa for support. "You saw what went on in the graveyard last night. Do you two really think it's a good idea to mess with this stuff? We don't know what we're doing, and much as you want to think you're an expert, Carson, you're not. And that makes this a really stupid idea." She wrapped her arms around herself and shivered a little bit.

"I thought you don't believe in ghosts." Teresa took a swig from her bottled water. Her eyebrows came together and she tilted her head to one side. "So what's the big deal?"

"I never said I don't believe in ghosts," Rachel retorted, meeting my eyes. "I said there wasn't conclusive proof they exist. That's different."

I swallowed. The look on her face—I'd never seen her look like that before. She'd been standing next to me at the cemetery, she'd touched my back for herself and felt how cold it had been on a warm and moist evening.

Maybe—*maybe* I hadn't been the only one who'd felt something. Our eyes met and she looked away immediately.

"It's going to be perfectly safe," Carson was saying. "For one thing, it's daytime—paranormal activity is very rare during the day." His tone was patronizing. "And, besides, ghosts can't hurt you physically. The worst they can do is scare you." He shrugged.

"Famous last words," Logan joked, a big grin on his face. He widened his eyes and in a hushed, scared voice went on, "Isn't that what they always say in the movies before something bad happens?" He clapped his hand over his mouth and rolled his eyes.

"You know, there's no rule that says you always *have* to act like a jackass." Rachel scowled at him.

He just stuck his tongue out at her.

"And there's five of us, anyway—if Rachel comes with, that is." Carson gave her a nasty smile.

She held up her hands. "I never said I wasn't going to go. I just said it's a bad idea. You all don't have to jump all over me."

"Besides, we're just going to go look around in the woods." Carson acted like no one else had said anything, addressing his remarks to Rachel. "As long as we keep an eye out for snakes"— Teresa made a gulping sound at this—"we should be fine. We're just making sure, you know, that it was just a weird dream, right, Scotty?"

I forced a smile on my face. "Yeah. I mean, this is just to make me feel better so I can sleep tonight." I took a deep breath and stood up. "So what are we waiting for?"

Teresa walked over to the door. "Let me get us all some bottled water," she suggested. "It feels like it's going to just keep getting hotter, and we don't know how long we'll be exploring, right?"

Once she came back out and passed everyone a perspiring bottle of cold water, we walked through the lodge to the door leading out to the parking lot. Mrs. Bartlett and Annie were clearing away the buffet, and Logan paused for a second, looking over at Annie before Teresa shoved him and he started walking again. We went back outside and crossed the parking lot to where the path emerged from the woods. I didn't look back, just kept walking until I reached the tree line. I stopped and looked back. They were all standing on the pavement, hadn't even started heading down the path across the lawn. "Are you coming? Or do you want me to do this by myself?"

One by one, they started up the path. I stood aside and let them pass me, falling into step with Rachel in the back. "You sure you're okay?" I asked her, keeping my voice down. Logan and Carson were leading the way, Logan talking and laughing loudly the way he always did. "You seem—"

"I didn't sleep well." She brushed a lock of hair out of her face and didn't look at me. "I'm tired and not in the mood for Carson's bullshit, if you must know." She gave me a brittle smile. "I probably should have just stayed in bed."

I didn't say anything.

"No, I didn't have bad dreams, if that's what you're wondering." It was like she was reading my mind. "I just couldn't fall asleep. I don't know why. Last night was just creepy, okay?"

"You didn't…" I fumbled for words. "Last night…"

She stopped walking and gave me an angry look. "I didn't feel anything, okay?" Her voice shook, but her eyes were determined. "Nothing. Do you understand me?"

Her vehemence startled me. "There's nothing to be afraid of—"

"Not a goddamned thing." She started walking faster, catching up to Teresa, and they started talking animatedly.

I stood there for a moment before starting to walk again myself. Logan and Carson were waiting at the fork, Logan leaning on the sign. When they saw me coming, they headed down the path leading deeper into the woods.

After the fork, the path started going down a slight slope. The trees formed a canopy of limbs over our heads, so we weren't in direct sunlight even though the blue sky was visible through the thickly knit branches from time to time. It was quiet in the woods, other than the slight hum of insects and the occasional chirping of birds. There were also some big rocks embedded in the dirt in places. The rocks were covered with green moss, which was kind of slippery, and I found myself having to grab for branches or tree trunks occasionally when my feet slipped and started to go out from under me.

The forest was beautiful, pristine and still and green. Every so often a bird would soar by just overhead, heading from one tree to another. In places, the growth of bushes and fledgling trees almost hid the path from view, and I had to push branches out of the way to get through. The majority of the trees closest to the path were small and young, the trees getting bigger and thicker the farther they were from the path, and it occurred to me that the path must have been much wider at some point, more like a dirt road than the narrow path it was now. Every once in a while, we had to climb over a rotting fallen tree, beetles and other bugs crawling along the surface of its brittle, fragile bark. But the air was so fresh and clean, with the scent of flowers I couldn't identify and pinesap and maple. I turned and looked behind me, and there was no sign of the road or anything other than forest. We walked into a small clearing at one point, and I saw a deer, frozen in place and staring at us before it turned and bounded away, disappearing into the trees in a matter of seconds. There was a small creek lazily twisting through that clearing, so narrow it was easy to step over and so shallow and clear I could see the rocks on the bottom.

I stepped over and followed the others back into the woods. I pulled out my phone and started taking pictures of everything—the trees, bushes, moss—one after the other, as quickly as my phone could snap. I was starting to sweat a bit, the underarms of my T-shirt getting damp as I slapped at mosquitoes and horseflies when they landed on my bare skin.

I don't know when the feeling really started, to be honest, but I went around a curve and saw an enormous tree just off to the side on the right, whose trunk split into two enormous branches jutting up toward the sky about five feet over my head, other heavy branches shooting out of the separated trunk. There was a knothole in the trunk, maybe about a foot below where the trunk split. As I raised my phone to take a picture—

—I was looking into the knothole, and it wasn't far over my head but only just above my eye level, and the path was, in fact, a lot wider, and there was a folded piece of paper inside the tree, and I was filled with joy as I grabbed it and pulled it out, unfolding it—

I was startled back into the present when I heard Logan shouting. I looked ahead and I realized I couldn't see them—they'd gotten far ahead of me while I was standing there looking at the split tree. With one last glance at it, I started hurrying along the path. It took another turn to the left after about twenty yards or so, and I kept walking as fast as I could, not wanting to run because the ground was still damp and slippery. I caught myself as the ground—and the path—began sloping sharply downward. I almost slipped, grabbing onto a branch to catch myself, and I took a deep breath.

Everything seemed so familiar.

I could see Rachel and Teresa ahead of me on the path, and they both waved me to come on. As I came closer to them, I realized that while the path itself continued to wind down, the ground to my left ended in a sharp cliff, and just beyond it, on a plateau or shelf where the ground leveled off into another big clearing, was something that looked like—

"Is that a roof?" I said as I caught up to them.

"It's not a good idea to get separated from us in the woods," Teresa replied with a frown. "And, yes, it's some kind of building—a cabin."

The small building had collapsed inward on itself at some point. It was made of wood, and in places where the building had collapsed the wood had split and splintered. The clearing wasn't clear anymore—small young trees were growing everywhere, but so were rotten old gray stumps. "Carson and Logan went looking around," Rachel said. "They told us to wait here for you."

"You don't think anyone lives there, do you?" I asked, feeling a weird sense of déjà vu, like I'd been there before.

But it looked different now.

They both looked at me like I'd lost my mind. "Well, unless the person who does doesn't care about electricity or access to the road, I'd say no one lives there." Teresa smiled at me, rolling her eyes a little bit. "No, it looks abandoned. It doesn't look like anyone's lived here in about a million years."

"I meant like a hobo or a tramp."

But as I looked at the wrecked cabin—and at the trees beyond, and heard the sound of water rushing—the sense of familiarity grew stronger and stronger. I walked past them and saw there were mossy round stones set out, leading from the path to what would have been the front door of the cabin at one point. A horsefly flew right past my face, and I swatted at it with a shudder as I pushed my way through the tree shoots and bushes that had grown up along the stone path. I saw the green baseball cap Logan was wearing over the collapsed building—he was looking around behind it. In the front of the wreckage were rosebushes gone wild, covered with dying and rotting blooms.

I froze and almost gagged.

The place smelled of *death*.

There was another, smaller collapsed structure on the side far from me, rotting wood collapsed in a big heap.

It's the well, for water.

The cabin or whatever it may have been at one time was small, far smaller than the cabin my family was staying in. If it had ever been painted at any point in its history, the paint had peeled away years ago. The wood was rotting, and from the angle the roof was sitting at it looked like it had probably collapsed under the weight of snow during a brutal winter sometime years ago. As I stood there, Logan and Carson moved into my sight—

—and everything changed.

I shook my head and rubbed my eyes.

I couldn't be seeing what I was seeing.

Was I losing my mind?

The cabin was no longer a ruin. It looked new, built from strong and sturdy wood, and I could almost smell the raw timber. The roof was solid. The well looked like any other working well would, a round brick base with a wooden cover and a wooden crossbeam, with a rope wrapped around it and a bucket hanging. Even the trees seemed different somehow—the smaller ones were nowhere to be seen, and the stumps looked raw, like the trees had only recently been chopped down. All of the underbrush was gone, and the rosebushes were short, maybe only a foot high, and the sweet smell of the recently bloomed red roses filled my nose.

It was a perfect little place to live.

As I stood there gaping, I heard someone coming down the path through the woods. I turned—there was no sign of either Rachel or Teresa anywhere, it was like they had simply vanished into thin air—and a young man came into view from the woods, coming down the path. He was wearing dark brown pants, and his dark reddish-brown hair hung loose and tangled to his shoulders. He wasn't wearing a shirt, and the sun shone through the trees on his tanned, firm skin that glistened with sweat. His skin was covered in freckles, and he was smiling. He was carrying an ax, and once he reached the level of the clearing, he walked over to a woodpile behind the cabin that hadn't been there just a moment before, when things had been different, passing so close to me I could have touched him if I hadn't been too terrified to reach out and touch him, and I watched as he swung the ax and lodged it in the center of a big stump.

I've lost my mind, I thought in horror.

He looked just like Marc.

This was just like my dream in the car yesterday, when I dozed off on our way up the mountain. *But I'm not dreaming now. What's happening to me?*

Logan and Carson were nowhere to be seen, either.

I felt a scream rising in my throat but I fought it down.

My heart started racing, and I put my hand against a tree to keep myself from falling as my knees buckled.

What the hell was happening?

As I leaned against the tree, the young man, whoever he was, started chopping wood, the muscles in his back flexing as he swung the ax and the wood splintered.

I felt drawn to him somehow, as though I should know who he was, and once the dizziness and panic passed, I felt an overwhelming sense of love.

Albert, I wonder if he's Albert.

I don't know how long I stood there, watching him, the gentle warm breezes of spring—*how do you know it's spring*—bringing the scent of wildflowers and honeysuckle to my nose. Bees were buzzing as they flew from flower to flower, and the silence was encompassing, like a blanket wrapped around me. The only sound was the ax whistling through the air as he swung it, the sound of the wood splintering, and his grunts as he raised the ax and swung it again.

"Scotty? Are you all right?"

I shook my head again and was back in the present.

Teresa and Rachel were both staring at me, their faces concerned.

"I'm fine." I ran my shaking hands through my hair. *I'm just losing my fucking mind, is all.* I took a deep breath and saw something out of the corner of my eye. Carson was kneeling next to the wreckage of the well, trying to see down inside it. He looked up at us.

"It's been sealed." He shrugged. "I guess it would be dangerous to leave it open."

I couldn't see Logan anywhere. I closed my eyes and could vividly see the young man in my mind as clearly as I had just a moment ago.

He looked so much like Marc...

"I've been talking to you for about five minutes now," Teresa said in a hushed voice. "Are you sure you're all right?"

"You were like in a trance or something," Rachel added. "Just staring off into space like we weren't even here." She licked her lips. "And your face..." Her voice trailed off. She was pale, her eyes wide.

She looks terrified, and for that matter, so does Teresa. What just happened here? How can I possibly explain what just happened without sounding completely insane? How, when even I had no idea what it was?

"My mind just wandered." I gave them what I hoped was a reassuring smile. "I got lost in thought, I guess. Sorry."

"Uh-uh." Teresa shook her head. "I'm not buying it. Maybe we should take you down to town to see a doctor. I'm sure there's an emergency clinic or something—"

"Absolutely not!" I snapped, feeling a little queasy. I swallowed and took some deep breaths. "I told you, I'm fine. Forget about it, okay?"

I walked past them and over to where Logan was kneeling by the wreckage of the old well. "What are you looking for?" I asked when I reached him. He hadn't moved since I—

lost my mind for just a minute before coming back to my senses?

—had reached the clearing. He was still kneeling there on the ground, staring down into the blackness through a hole in the wooden planks that had been nailed down to cover the hole. Even though the structure over the well had collapsed at some point in the past, the wreckage didn't completely cover the planks. I frowned. In my vision or whatever the hell that had been, there had been a low brick wall forming the base of the well, but there was no sign of it now.

So it wasn't a vision or anything, it was a weird daydream. Your mind just went somewhere else and created a whole scene from the reality of what your eyes were seeing. You invented a well like wells you've seen before, but there couldn't have been a brick wall like you imagined because it would still be here, and if they took the bricks down they wouldn't have left the rest of the structure here, covering it so haphazardly, it's kind of dangerous the way it is, anyone could stumble or trip and fall down the well.

Great. I was convincing myself that I was going crazy.

And what about yesterday's dream?

Logan looked up and smiled. "Not looking for anything, really." He stood up and wiped his hands on the sides of his shorts. "I was just trying to see if I could tell how deep it was. I felt like…" He shrugged. "I just had this really weird sense about it, is all. It doesn't make sense, I know."

I stared at him, wondering. I turned to see Carson stepping over the threshold into the wrecked cabin—

And I remembered doing the same thing. The door was unpainted, and it was open. The windows were also open, and the plain white curtains danced in the soft breeze. The inside of the cabin was just one big open room. The floor was unvarnished, raw wood. In one corner was a fireplace and next to it was a wood-burning stove. Cast-iron pots and pans hung neatly on the wall next to the stove, and there were several iron buckets on the floor beneath them. There wasn't much furniture. In a far corner of the room, a small pallet was made up as a sleeping area. A large wooden trunk with a flat lid had some books stacked on top of it. There was a table made from raw wood with two small chairs made from the same wood. A lantern sat in the center of the table. The place smelled masculine, of sweat and hard work, and slightly of sawdust...

"Carson Wolfe, are you completely *insane?*" Rachel shouted. "Come back out here right this minute!"

How can I be remembering any of this? I rubbed my eyes and leaned against the trunk of a tree. I felt tired, maybe a little nauseous.

Carson stuck his head back out through the doorway, that I'm-up-to-something grin on his face, his eyebrows arched up almost all the way to his hairline. "This looks like a place kids come to party," he said, tossing out a filthy whiskey bottle. "Lots of empty chip bags, beer cans, and liquor bottles."

"I can't imagine anyone coming to this place," Rachel sniffed, wrinkling her nose. "Out in the middle of nowhere, and disgusting."

"Out in the middle of nowhere is probably part of the appeal," Logan pointed out. He stood back up, wiping his hands on his shorts. "No one would think of coming looking for kids here." He pointed to a rock circle with long-dead embers in the center. "You come up here to camp out, build a fire right there—and hang out and get drunk all night long."

"You'd think the Bartletts would notice the smoke," Teresa said. She turned to me and said in a low whisper, "Are you okay, Scotty? You look kind of green."

I closed my eyes and knelt down, taking some deep breaths. I didn't feel very good, to be honest. The nausea was getting worse and coming in horrible waves, each wave progressing stronger than the one before. My eyes were burning, my head was starting to hurt, and my stomach was churning.

The well—it has everything to do with the well.

"I don't—feel so hot," I said out loud and got another flash of the shirtless man, standing in the doorway with a big smile on his face.

And as everything went dark, I heard the voice calling again.

"Berrrrrrrrrrrrrrrrrrrrrrrrrrr-tiiiiiiiiiiiiiieeeeeeeeeeeee."

CHAPTER SEVEN

The black began to fade.

It was like being underwater, like I was at the bottom of a darkened swimming pool and I could look up and see the sunlight shining on the surface of the water. I started to make my way upward toward the light. The pressure in my lungs was building and I needed air, I was almost there, almost...

I opened my eyes and found myself staring up at four pale, wide-eyed faces.

Carson let out an explosive sigh, as their concerned faces all seemed to relax in relief. "Are you okay, man?" he asked, reaching down to touch my forehead with the back of his hand. "No fever—if anything, his skin feels cool."

"I'm fine." I could see the sky above them, through the tops of trees, clear blue and bright sunshine. "I don't know what happened. Did I pass out?"

"Dude, you scared the shit out of us," Logan said after a moment, the relief clearly showing in his face. "Your eyes just rolled up in the back of your head and you went down like a ton of bricks. Your skin looked *green*." He peered down at me. "You're getting your color back now."

"Sorry—didn't mean to scare you guys." I tried to sit up, but everything started spinning and I got dizzy and a little nauseous. "Whoa, maybe I'd better lie here for a little bit more." I lay back down, putting my hands behind my head. I closed my eyes and took some deep breaths.

"Here, drink some water," Teresa said. I opened my eyes and she passed me her water bottle, her hand shaking slightly. I came up on my elbow and took the water from her, and took a drink. I was really thirsty, and I gulped down the water until the bottle was completely empty. "Sorry," I handed it back to her. "Where's mine? And my phone?"

"You dropped your water." Rachel's voice was faint and a little shaky. "But I picked up your phone." She gave me a weak smile and handed me my phone.

I slipped the phone in my pocket, closed my eyes, took a deep breath, and sat up. I wasn't dizzy anymore—the nausea and the headache were also gone. "Is there any more water?" I asked, and Carson handed me another half-empty plastic bottle. I took a long pull on the water and handed it back to him. "I feel a lot better now," I said, smiling at them. I shivered, but then felt like my blood was flowing again. "Sorry if I scared you. I don't know what happened, I really don't. But I'm better now, really."

They exchanged concerned glances, and Teresa gulped a bit.

"What is it?" I asked, looking at each one of them in turn, trying to read their facial expressions. "What aren't you telling me?"

Carson cleared his throat. "Okay, um, while you were unconscious"—his voice broke, and he took another deep breath before he continued—"you were *talking*."

"It was creepy," Rachel said, shuddering. "Really creepy."

"Talking?" A chill went down my spine, and I swallowed down the fear that was growing inside of me. "What do you mean, talking? I thought I passed out—how could I be talking if I was passed out?"

Teresa knelt down beside me and took my hand in both of hers. "Don't get upset or freak out, okay? Just stay calm, will you promise me that?" When I nodded, she went on. "Okay, I'll tell you what happened." She looked at Carson, who nodded, and she turned back to me. "You just went down. I mean, Rachel and I were behind you, but you just collapsed and fell." She shuddered as she remembered. "It was freaky, your phone and your water went flying. And you were lying there, moaning and crying, and you kept saying—" She took a deep breath. "Over and over, you kept saying *can't be dead, can't be dead, can't be dead.*"

Can't be dead, can't be dead.

I shook my head, biting my lip. "What does that mean?" I could hear hysteria in my voice, and I closed my eyes again, taking some deep breaths.

I'm losing my mind, isn't that what it means?

"The worst part was you screamed right before you opened your eyes." Rachel's voice was shaking. "Oh my God, it was the most awful thing I've ever heard in my life." Her eyes were full of tears, and she covered her face with her hands. "It was so loud..."

Teresa forced out a cold laugh. "Yeah, it echoed all through the forest, and you scared off all the birds. They really took off, got the hell out of Dodge." She looked up and around. "It was really bloodcurdling," she went on in a soft voice. "I've never heard anything like that—and I hope I never do again, no offense."

Logan put an arm around her shoulders and squeezed, and she put her head down on his shoulder. "Do you remember anything at all that happened while you were passed out?" he asked gently.

I took a deep breath. "No. I don't remember anything. But I remember"—I paused—"I felt like I was underwater, you know how you can go to the bottom of a pool and open your eyes and you can see the sun shining on the surface? It was—it was like that. And I had to get to the surface. And when I did, I woke up." I shook my head. "I don't know how else to explain it to you guys."

"Something happened *before* you passed out, didn't it?" Teresa said, peering down at my face. "Something's been going on with you ever since we left the lodge this morning. Come on, Scotty, you have to tell us. We can't help you if we don't know what's going on with you, and we want to help you." When I didn't answer, she turned to the others. "I saw his face before he went out. His eyes were glassy. He was looking at me, but through me, like I wasn't there." She shuddered. "I kept saying his name, and nothing—no reaction, no nothing. You saw it, didn't you, Logan?"

Logan nodded.

"Scotty, what's the last thing you remember before you passed out?" Rachel asked softly. "Dude, it was like you were in a trance."

"I don't..." I looked at each of their faces. "I don't know how to explain it to you guys without sounding completely insane."

"Scotty, you're not crazy." Carson whispered. "We were all there in the cemetery last night, okay? And you dreamed about coming into the woods last night, remember? You heard a voice calling Bertie—and we all heard it just now, before you passed out."

"You…you heard it, too?" I stared at him, completely shocked. He nodded, and as I looked at each one of them in turn, they all nodded, too.

"It was…awful." Rachel shuddered. "It was just like you described it this morning. Hollow and sad and mournful. It didn't really scare me—it just made me feel, I don't know, really sad. Like you said you felt in the cemetery last night."

"There's something going on," Carson went on. "I don't know what it is, but it's something paranormal." He didn't seem triumphant or smug to be proven right. "But now we've all experienced it in some way. And right after the voice, that was when you passed out. The voice was the last of it, though." He rubbed his head. "When you got down to the clearing, I could see you from where I was, on the side of the cabin here." He gestured to the ruins. "You froze. Completely froze, like the girls said. Your eyes were all glassy, and they were talking to you, but you weren't there." He licked his lips. "And then you seemed to come out of it, and you walked over to where Logan was, next to the well…and then we heard the voice and you went out."

"Do you remember anything at all?" Teresa whispered.

What the hell, if I can't trust them who can I trust? I took a deep breath. "It's like I was there, but I wasn't. I know that doesn't make sense, it doesn't make sense to me. One minute I was walking down the path"—I looked over at the path—"and the next thing I knew, I was still there, but I wasn't *there*, everything was different. The well, for one thing, it wasn't broken down the way it is now, it looked like a well, you know, with a round brick base and the little roof and the crossbeam with the rope, and the cabin…" I explained, slowly and carefully, everything I'd seen.

But something told me not to tell them the young man looked like Marc, so I didn't. Or that I'd dreamed it all before. That was too much.

When I finished, I shrugged. "So, what do you think? Am I going crazy?"

"No, you're not going crazy," Carson said quickly before anyone else could respond. "I think...we encountered something like this on the show."

"Here we go," Rachel muttered, rolling her eyes.

"Just because you don't believe doesn't mean it's not possible or true," Carson retorted angrily. "So you'd rather just believe Scotty's going crazy and have him locked up in the nuthouse? And how do you explain the voice on the recording? The voice we just heard? Can you explain that?" He folded his arms and actually started tapping his foot. "I'm waiting."

"I didn't say Scotty's going crazy, asshole," Rachel snapped. "But there are other possibilities besides the supernatural, you know."

"Nobody's locking Scotty away in a nuthouse," Teresa snapped. "Just let him finish, Rachel, before we decide what to do, okay?" Rachel made a face but nodded. "Go on."

"As I was saying"—Carson glared at his sister for a moment—"one of the houses we investigated on the show this past summer was in Northern California, and before this particular family moved into it, no one had the slightest idea that the house was haunted. But their teenaged daughter—within a week of moving into the house, she started acting really strangely. Walking in her sleep, talking in her sleep to the point where her family could actually have conversations with her that she wouldn't remember when she woke, and they swore the person they were talking to wasn't their daughter."

"Was she possessed?" Teresa managed to keep her voice neutral, but disbelief was clearly written all over her face.

"In a way, but not the way you think—not like *The Exorcist,* you know, a demon or the devil or whatever it was." Carson replied with a scowl, totally serious. "There was a restless spirit trapped in the house—she died in the house when she was the same age as the family's daughter, Ruth. Well, she was *murdered* in the house when she was the same age." He pushed his glasses up. "Look, I don't pretend like I know everything—no one does. All we can do is theorize based on the evidence"—Rachel snorted at this, but didn't say anything—"that we do have, but the general consensus among parapsychologists is that ghosts are simply souls that can't move on because, I don't know, they have unfinished business? This girl in the California house, she was raped and murdered by a previous owner, and she eventually led them to where her body had been buried on the property. Once she'd been buried properly, the hauntings stopped."

"You're right, you didn't explain that well," Logan said with a shake of his head. "So, basically you're saying this ghost in California was haunting that house because she hadn't had a proper burial? What about countries where burial customs are different? Wouldn't all those souls be trapped, if they needed to be buried?" When we all stared at him, he shrugged. "I took a Comparative Religion class last year. It was interesting."

"I said I don't know all the answers—no one does." Carson glared at Logan. "But there's also a theory that the afterlife—what happens to the soul after we die—is directly tied to what we believe in while we are alive." He shrugged. "Maybe what we experience after we die is completely based on what we believe, who knows? When you're a spirit—"

"So what you're saying is Albert has some unfinished business here?" *Tell them about the young man you saw.* I leaned back against the tree. "And for some reason, he's using me to finish it? I don't see how that explains what just happened here. And he is buried—we all saw his grave."

Carson flushed. "Ruth—the girl in California—the same thing that's happening to you also happened to *her.* She was getting flashes of memory from the murdered girl, seeing the house the way it had been when the dead girl had lived there, that sort of thing. And when it would happen, her eyes would go glassy, and she wouldn't hear people talking to her. Sometimes she'd go into a dead faint when it was over, just like you did." He turned and looked at the ruined cabin. "My guess is that this place is important somehow to Albert, and he was trying to show you something. Are you sure you told us everything you saw?"

I bit my lip. For some reason, I couldn't do it. I just couldn't tell them the young man I saw looked like Marc. "I think so. I mean, I'm pretty sure. If I think of anything else I'll tell you." *Why won't you tell them about Marc? Don't you think it's important? Are you afraid if you tell him the guy you saw looked like Marc they'll think it's some gay fantasy of yours? They'll laugh at you? They're your friends, Scotty. Don't be afraid of them.*

But I didn't say anything.

"We need to know who this cabin belonged to," Carson went on. "Since it's on the lodge property, I'm sure the Bartletts probably know something about it. Someone lived here—you can tell." He swept his arm around. "Rosebushes, a well…yeah, someone lived here." He beamed at them. "And I'd be willing to bet a million dollars someone lived here when Albert was alive."

"I think we should talk to Aunt Arlene and Uncle Hank," Rachel insisted. "If you're wrong, and there's something medical wrong with him—and before you bite my head off, brother dear, I'm not saying that a medical problem precludes paranormal activity, okay? But wouldn't that be part of the process?" She smiled triumphantly at her brother, who was sputtering. "Just because I didn't intern on the show doesn't mean I don't ever watch it, you know. And your Ruth—she had a complete medical exam, complete with a brain scan to make sure there wasn't something physically wrong with her, didn't she?"

"She has a point," Teresa said. "We have to rule out medical causes."

"And the voice could have been a collective hallucination," Rachel continued. "We have to tell Aunt Arlene and Uncle Hank. If something's really wrong with Scotty, and we didn't tell them—I don't want to be responsible for that. I mean, for all we know, he could have a brain tumor or something. We don't know. We're not doctors." She flung a hand out. "And this is crazy. Carson, I'm sorry. I know you want to believe in the paranormal and all, but do you have any idea how crazy all of this sounds? Could you imagine the reaction we'd get from our parents if we tried to explain all of this to them? They'd have us all locked up in a psych ward."

"Sorry, bro," Logan playfully punched Carson in the arm. "But I gotta agree with Rache. We are so in over our heads here."

"I don't want anyone to say anything to my parents," I said. They all looked at me. "I don't. I think I'd know if I had a brain tumor or not, and a brain tumor didn't make my back cold last night in the cemetery, and it wasn't a brain tumor that made me walk out into the woods last night, and it wasn't a brain tumor that made that flag wave in the cemetery, either." I crossed my arms. "I don't know how to explain it to you all to make you understand, but I think I'd know if I was losing my mind or if—if I was sick." I shook my head. "None of this happened before yesterday. How could that be if I was sick? Or going crazy? Wouldn't I have had symptoms before I got to North Hollow?"

"He has a point," Teresa replied. "Seriously. Why don't we do this?" She turned to Carson. "Let's see what we can find out to maybe prove Carson's right—or wrong, for that matter. It can't hurt to do some research about Albert, the Tylers, and this cabin. And Rachel, if you want to you can do some research on brain diseases, see if any of this can be explained as symptoms of some kind of illness—and not just physical." She looked at me and smiled sadly. "Sorry, Scotty, but we have to consider the other side of it, too. You may be having a breakdown. Maybe somehow *you* caused the voice we all heard—the voice your mother heard, too. And after a few days, if Carson can't prove any of his theory, then we have to tell the adults. Are we all agreed?" The others nodded.

"It sounds fair." Carson agreed.

"Don't I have a say in any of this?" I asked. "I mean, come on, guys, you're making decisions about me without any input from me? How is that fair?"

Teresa smiled at me, and patted my leg. "Sorry, Scotty, but we have to operate under the assumption that you're not in your right mind, one way or another." When no one said anything, she looked at her watch. "I say we get out of here. We've made some good progress." She looked over at the ruined cabin. "And for the record, Carson—I do think you're right. We just have to cover every base."

She had a point. She was going to make a good lawyer one day.

We walked back up the trail in silence. I looked back at the cabin, and felt *–sorrow, sadness*—and then it was gone in just a moment.

I knew I wasn't losing my mind.

The cabin *meant* something.

"You know something," I said slowly as we reached the fork in the path and started to walk away from the cabin, toward the lodge. "My mom thought someone was out calling their pet last night—we need to ask the Bartletts if anyone on the mountain has a pet named Bertie or something that sounds like that."

Carson scowled.

"If we're going to cover every base, we have to rule out that anyone was out calling, don't we?" I scowled back at him. "And you know, we also have to consider the possibility that this whole thing is all a set up of some sort." I shrugged. "I mean, someone could be playing an elaborate trick." I crossed my arms. "I mean, maybe the Bartletts know about your dad's show about the paranormal. Maybe they want to get their lodge on a national television show. It's free publicity, isn't it?"

"Excellent point, Scotty." Teresa nodded. "People have done crazier things than this to get on television."

"They don't strike me as the type, but you're absolutely right." Carson was practically dancing in place. "We have to consider everything, and not until everything else is ruled out can we determine that whatever's happening is supernatural in origin."

"In that case, we also have to consider the possibility that Scotty's involved," Logan pointed out. He grinned at me sheepishly. "If we have to consider everything, we have to, sorry. I mean, I don't think you'd do something like that, but we have to think about it."

"Uh huh." I nodded, my cheeks flaming. *Some vacation—my friends are considering the options that I might be insane, or have a brain tumor, or am involved in some elaborate scam. Great.*

No one said another word as we continued walking back through the woods to the lodge. It was getting hotter, and my hair was damp with sweat. Going down the path, too, had been a lot easier than hiking its steady upward slope. By the time we reached the tree line just outside the parking lot, we were all breathing a little harder and soaking with sweat. "Thank God," Rachel breathed as we made it out of the woods. "I was beginning to think I wasn't going to make it." She emptied what was left in her water bottle into her mouth.

As we stood there, the back door to the kitchen opened and Annie Bartlett emerged, carrying a bag of trash out to the big Dumpster out by the shed. "Annie!" Logan shouted and took off running.

Annie's face lit up as she watched Logan run up to her, and I felt bad for her. *She's fallen for him already,* I thought sadly.

"I know about the cabin but I don't know anything about it," she was saying as we walked up. "When Mom and Dad bought the place, the agent showed it to them, of course, but it's in such bad shape, and there's no sewer or power out there, and no road, so they decided to just leave it as it is and not bother with it. The well's dried up, too." She shrugged her small shoulders. "I know some kids like to go hang out there and drink, you know, because no one ever goes out there, but I never go out there." She shuddered. "There's something about that place I don't like."

I noticed that as she spoke Rachel got a smug look on her face and wondered what she was thinking.

"Who'd your parents buy the lodge from, Annie?" This was Teresa, and her voice was friendly.

"Why do you care?"

"Just curious."

"The people who owned the place before we did retired—they were pretty old." Annie made a face. "I think they moved to Florida, and Mom and Dad were tired of city life, so here we are."

"There aren't any stories about the place being haunted, are there?" This was from Carson.

My mind was already starting to wander. I was sweating, and I was thirsty. I moved away from the group and went into the lodge through the front door. The lodge wasn't air-conditioned—there were window units in the rooms—and all the windows were open. I could see the lake sparkling in the sun at the end of the long sloping lawn. I walked over to the cooler, retrieved a Coke, and went out onto the porch that ran the length of the building on the lake side. I sat down in a wooden rocking chair and put my feet up on the unfinished railing.

Was I losing my mind? I had to consider the possibility, even if I didn't believe it was possible nor did I like the very idea. Was I having a breakdown of sorts? I pulled my cell phone out of my pocket. I really missed Marc and wished he was here with me. Was this some kind of weird reaction to the pressures of coming out to everyone, and missing Marc?

When I'd seen the young man in my vision or whatever the hell it was I'd had out in the woods, I'd felt so happy. I knew that feeling quite well—it was the same feeling I had whenever I saw Marc if I hadn't seen him for a few days, like when his family went away to visit relatives at Thanksgiving or Christmas. It was how I'd feel when I saw him after we got back to Farmington. I—or Albert—had feelings for that guy.

Is that why you didn't say anything to the others about him looking like Marc? Because you didn't want to bring up the gay thing?

What Carson had said about that haunting in California—what if I was the first gay kid the right age to stop at Albert's grave since he was buried? That was a connection between us, a strong enough connection for him to do whatever it was he was doing to me. Maybe that was why I'd felt so emotional at his grave. Maybe that's why I heard someone calling him last night in the woods.

I sat up, almost spilling my Coke in the process.

Someone was calling him. We'd all heard it, hadn't we? Even Mom had heard it.

But who?

"There you are," Teresa said from behind me. The screen door slammed shut behind her, and she sat down in the chair on the other side of the table from me. She popped the top on a Diet Coke and leaned back in her chair. "How are you doing, really, Scotty?"

I shrugged. "I'm fine. Did Annie have anything interesting to say?"

She shook her head. "No, she doesn't know anything. Carson and Logan went off to talk to her parents. Rachel's back in the game room looking stuff up on the Internet." She sighed. "Are you sure, Scotty? You can talk to me, you know." She reached over and touched my hand. "You've been so withdrawn since we got here—what's going on?"

I looked into her brown eyes and smiled back at her. "Well, this whole Albert ghost thing hasn't exactly helped, you know." I took a deep breath. "I was pretty nervous about coming here, seeing everyone again." I turned to look back at the shimmering surface of the lake. "I mean, no one answered my e-mail."

"Scotty, I can't speak for anyone else, but I didn't answer because I figured it would be easier to talk in person." She let go of my hand and started rocking in her chair. "You're still Scotty. Who cares if you like boys or girls?"

"Thanks." I bit my lower lip and felt tears coming to my eyes. "That means a lot."

"I mean, I worry about you—there are a lot of assholes in the world." She went on like I hadn't spoken at all. She smiled at me. "But you're a good guy. You're smart and good looking and funny and you have a great personality. None of that is different. Anyone who wants to judge you for who you're attracted to is someone not worth knowing, you know? Besides, I always kind of wondered about you."

"You did not."

"Oh, yes I did." She laughed. "Come on, you might have thought you were being sly, but I saw you looking at boys on the beach last summer."

"There were some hot ones." I sighed and leaned back in my chair. "Thanks, Teresa, it means a lot."

"I'm kind of worried about all of this stuff going on, too," she said, taking another swig of her soda and muffling a belch with her hand. "I know you're not going crazy, but are you sure you don't want to go see a doctor?"

I turned and looked at her. "Teresa, I know there's nothing wrong with me physically. I can't explain how I know, I just *do.*" I hesitated. "There's, um, a couple things I didn't share with everyone about what happened in the woods."

An eyebrow went up. "I knew you were holding something back. Spill. I won't tell anyone else unless you want me to."

I took a deep breath and told her about the dream I had in the car and the guy I saw both times, describing him, in detail, as well as the powerful emotional response I'd had.

She whistled. "You think it was Albert?"

I shook my head. "I don't. I think Carson's right. I think I'm somehow getting flashes of his memory." I rubbed my eyes. "It sounds so fucking crazy! But I think that guy was, I don't know, important to Albert. He was in love with that guy. The way I felt when I saw him—it's the way I feel when I see my boyfriend."

"You have a boyfriend?" Her delight was written all over her face. "You didn't say anything about a boyfriend!" She leaned in. "Details. Just between us."

So, I told her about Marc, how we met, how we had to keep everything a secret from his awful father.

"He sounds dreamy." She closed her eyes. "Do you have a picture of him?"

I pulled out my wallet and showed her his junior class picture.

"Cute," she commented as I put it back in my pocket. She was about to say something else when the screen door opened and Logan and Carson joined us.

"You're not going to believe this." Carson was bouncing up and down on the balls of his feet. "The Tylers used to *own* this place. They actually built the lodge."

"Wow." Teresa winked at me. "Interesting!"

"They're mostly gone," Logan went on. "But there's still a Tyler living in North Hollow. And get this—she works at the North Hollow Historical Society." He held up the car keys. "Anyone up for a trip into town?"

CHAPTER EIGHT

"Cheer up, Rachel," Logan said as he started the engine, winking at her. "There's still plenty of time for Scotty to develop the symptoms of a brain tumor."

"You're such an asshole," Rachel said absently, not bothering to even look up from fiddling with her phone. "I never said I wanted him to have a brain tumor. Besides, we all agreed that we had to rule out a medical cause for what's happening, didn't we?" She glanced over at me and winked. "But we haven't ruled out schizophrenia."

I smothered a grin and winked back at her before crossing my eyes and tipping my head, letting my tongue roll out and hang to the side.

Teresa smacked my leg. "Stop it," she said, laughing.

I shrugged. "I figured a little laughter couldn't hurt, could it? I mean, I'm the one who might be going crazy."

Rachel had spent over an hour on the computer in the lodge's game room, going from link to link as she searched for any articles on any website, anywhere, that would give a medical cause for what I was experiencing. After Carson and Logan had told us about the Tylers, I'd gone back to my cabin—walking on the road because I didn't feel comfortable taking the shortcut through the woods by myself—to take another shower. I couldn't explain it, but I just didn't feel clean after our walk in the forest. When I'd gotten back, Logan and Carson were teasing Rachel mercilessly about her wish for me to have a brain tumor. Obviously, none of us really believed

Rachel wanted that, but joking and teasing was a great way to relieve the tension we were all feeling.

"If you're going crazy, we all are," Carson commented from the front seat over the stereo, which was blaring a One Direction song.

"How reassuring—maybe we can all get rooms on the same floor at the mental hospital," I said, leaning my head against the window glass as Logan started driving the SUV down the mountain. Teresa was sitting between Rachel and me, and she patted my leg as I touched the screen of my cell phone, waking it up. The word *Searching...* appeared in the upper left-hand corner as the little wheel spun slowly. After about a minute, *No Signal* replaced it.

I sighed and shoved it back into my shorts pocket.

At least when we got down to North Hollow, I'd be able to call or text Marc.

I looked back out the window as we headed down the mountain. I hadn't really been paying a lot of attention when we'd driven up to the lodge the day before, and of course, it had been dark when we'd gone down to the cemetery last night. But it was really beautiful.

There were mountaintops visible in almost every direction I could look, some of them dusted with snow at the very top. Every once in a while, the shoulder of the road was almost nonexistent, and I could see over the guardrail, down the side of the mountain, to a spectacular display of a waterfall throwing up mist that caught the sunlight, making little rainbows. As far as mountains went, these weren't that tall, really—we usually went skiing for a long weekend in Colorado every February, and those mountains certainly dwarfed those around Lake Thirteen—but that didn't make them any less beautiful to look at.

"Hey, there's the parents!" Logan swung the car off the road onto the narrow shoulder and braked. He slammed into park and hopped out. I opened my door and slid down. The guardrail was only a few inches away from where I was standing, and for a brief moment I was looking down an almost sheer drop of about twenty feet or so to where the clear rock-filled stream opened out into a wide pool of clear water. It seemed familiar—

—and everything changed again.

The pavement and guardrail weren't there anymore, and I was standing way too close to the edge. The road was dirt, not pavement, and the side I was so near was nothing more than a crumbling lip, with cracks and holes where the side had simply fallen away. I involuntarily took a step backward as vertigo made me dizzy. The trees and bushes were thicker than they had been just a moment ago, and above the sound of rushing water I heard a loud splash. Nervously, I took another step closer to the lip and looked over the side just as the young man I'd seen at the cabin surfaced in almost the direct center of the pool. He bobbed for a moment, wiping water out of his eyes. Then he stopped bobbing up and down, and only his torso from about the navel up was above water. He shook his head, the long hair flying from side to side, spraying drops of water in every direction. I could see a pile of clothing on the far side of the pool, right next to the water, and there was a path through the woods. The sun glistened on his broad shoulders as he walked to the far side of the pool, more of him emerging from the water as he got farther away from me, and I caught my breath as I saw enough of him exposed about the water to realize that he was naked—

"Scotty?" Teresa whispered urgently, tugging on my arm. "Are you okay? Did it happen again?"

Startled, I looked down. It was just as it had been when I'd first looked down. There was no one in the pool of water, no pile of clothes on the far shore, no path through the underbrush to the water's edge. I sighed and turned around. The gray SUV with all three sets of parents was pulled over on the other side of the road. Logan, Carson, and Rachel were standing around the driver's side door, and I could see my mother in the backseat through the window. I forced a smile on my face and nodded at Teresa. "I'm fine."

"What did you see?" she asked, not letting go of my arm.

"Nothing," I lied. "It just changed, that's all, and was different. I don't think it meant anything."

It meant something. You're getting flashes of memory. But who was that guy? He looked so much like Marc—that has to mean something.

But I didn't want to say anything about it to her—or to any of the others, for that matter.

I was shaking and I climbed back into the backseat, scooting over to the center to make room for Teresa. She shut the door behind her and took my hand.

"You're white as a sheet," she said, placing a hand on my forehead. "No fever, though, that's a good thing."

"I thought we already determined that it's not a brain tumor," I replied with a weak smile, which made her laugh. I leaned my head back and took some deep breaths.

"What did you see?" she asked again. "Scotty, you have to tell us. We can't help you if you don't tell us everything."

"It was like before," I closed my eyes, remembering. "The guardrail was gone, the road was dirt instead of pavement—and it made me nervous—the edge was all crumbling away. I heard a splash and looked down at the pool and everything was different. The air was different, like it was spring..." I focused, trying to remember. "Yes, I could smell blooming flowers, and it was warm, the sun was warm but there was a bit of a nip in the air, like, you know, spring. And I saw the guy again—the guy from the cabin, the one I saw earlier, he was getting out of the water and his clothes were all piled up on the shore and he was getting out of the water and he was..." I bit my lip. "Then you snapped me back into the present."

I heard the other SUV driving away, and a few moments later, everyone was getting back into our vehicle.

Logan started the engine again. "I told them we were going to look around the town and have lunch there," he said as he buckled his seat belt.

"Great," Teresa replied. "Scotty had another vision, or whatever it is he's been having." She squeezed my hand and winked to let me know my secret about seeing the young man naked was safe with her. "Nothing much, just a vision of the creek and the pool in some past time."

"That's so weird." Carson looked over the seat at us. "Are you sure that's all you saw? Albert must have wanted you to see it, that's why he showed it to you. You're sure that's it?"

"I don't know," I said, sharper than I'd intended. "Sorry." I shook my head. "This is just so damned frustrating. I don't know what he wants to tell me." I pounded my fist on my leg. "I wish he'd just tell me what he wants already!"

"I'm sure he wants to," Carson said calmly from the front seat. "He would if he could. But he can't. That's why we have to see what we can find out, so we can help him as much as we can."

I didn't answer, just kept looking out the window. About ten minutes later we passed the turn off to Cemetery Road, and Teresa squeezed my hand again. I got my phone back out just as we reached the bottom of the mountain, where Thirteenth Lake Road dead-ended into the state highway. Across the two lanes of pavement and about three yards of gravel and dirt was the upper Hudson River, at most a quarter mile across and looking choppy, the current moving fast. Little whitecaps occasionally showed up in the gray water, and some people in kayaks were moving across the surface of the river. Logan turned right after letting an eighteen-wheeler thunder past, and I watched as we passed a tire dealership, a gas station, and a sports-equipment rental place that also arranged white-water-rafting tours.

After about a mile, there was a road to the left, following the curve of the river. There was a sign that read North Hollow with an arrow pointing in that direction. *That's why I don't remember driving through town on the way here,* I thought as Logan slowed and turned to follow the two-lane road running alongside the river. And as we got farther away from the state highway, we reached the outskirts of the small town, evidenced by a sign announcing the city limits and the population—7640.

There was a pleasant little main street, with a big Walgreens and a Safeway sharing a big parking lot, and any number of small businesses—cafés, a locksmith, an auto mechanic, antique shops, a coffee shop, and an ice cream shop. We had just passed the small town-hall building when Carson said, "There's the historical society!"

Logan maneuvered the SUV into a parking spot in front of the North Hollow Historical Society building. It was a small building, made of wood and painted white with green shutters. There was a well-kept lawn, a small white picket fence running along the narrow sidewalk, and a big wooden sign painted brown with WELCOME TO THE NORTH HOLLOW HISTORICAL SOCIETY! OPEN MONDAY THRU SATURDAY FROM 12-5.

"What's our cover story?" Teresa asked after Logan had shut the engine off and we'd all gotten out. "We're not from around here. Don't you think Miss Alice Tyler is going to have some questions about why we're so interested in her family? Unless you plan on telling her that Scotty is communicating with one of her dead ancestors, of course. She won't think we're insane or anything."

"Leave it to me, I'll do all the talking," Carson replied with a smug little smile as he opened the gate and stepped aside. "After you."

I walked up the steps and opened the door. A bell rang as I walked inside. The air was slightly cooler inside than outside. Immediately to my right was a small table with a guestbook sitting open on it. There was a sign asking everyone to please sign in. I hesitated for a moment before stepping over and writing my name and address and the date in the spaces provided. I couldn't help but notice the last person to sign the book had done so the previous summer—obviously, the historical society wasn't a big tourist draw. I turned and walked into the main room.

There was a desk to one side facing the front door with a nameplate reading *Alice Tyler* on it. The desktop was completely bare, other than a computer monitor and a keyboard. There was a blue coffee mug with a big orange *S* on it in one corner with pens stuffed into it. A woman I assumed had to be Alice Tyler sat behind the desk, reading what appeared to be the *New York Times*. She looked up and smiled at us. She was in her fifties—maybe her sixties. Her graying dark hair was pulled back into a long braid that went down her back. She was wearing a floral print dress, and had bifocal glasses, which she pushed up the bridge of her nose. Her skin was a little loose and wrinkled, but her brown eyes were round and warm. I heard the door open and the bell ring again as everyone else came inside.

"Hi," I smiled back at her. "My name is Scotty Thompson and I'm staying—all of us are staying—up at Mohawk Lodge for the week. I was wondering if you could help us?"

"I'll do what I can," she replied. Her voice was as warm as her eyes, deep and friendly. "Are you interested in the area history? It's so nice when young people are interested in history."

"Great," Carson enthused. "I'm taking online classes—college prep, trying to get some credits while I'm still in high school—and I'm taking one from UCLA called 20th Century America." It was amazing how easily the lies rolled off his tongue—I had no idea Carson was such a good liar. "Anyway, I have to write a paper on any topic I want, and I thought it would be interesting to write one about the history of the lodge itself. After all, there's so much history in this area." His smile got wider. "And Annie—the girl who works there—suggested I should come here and talk to you, that it was your family that originally built the lodge. Can you help me?"

Her smile grew wider as he spoke, and when he was finished, she leaned back in her chair. "Annie's right, of course. It's true that my great-grandfather Benjamin Tyler bought the land and built the lodge over a hundred years ago."

She started talking, and to his credit, Carson pulled up a chair and started typing notes into his phone as she spoke. Teresa, Logan, and Rachel also pulled up chairs, but I was feeling antsy—I didn't want to sit down, and even though I was interested in whatever Miss Tyler had to say about the lodge's history, my mind was wandering. I started walking around, looking at the items hanging on the walls, looking in glass cases at arrowheads and tomahawks and colonial artifacts. I kept walking around—apparently North Hollow's big claim to fame was that there had been an Indian massacre near the beginning of the French and Indian War. There was even an old book under glass, which was apparently a history of the massacre, published sometime before World War II. Apparently, no other historian had found the area interesting enough to write about, because that was the only book in the entire place.

There was a doorway to another room, and I walked through it into a big room painted yellow. The curtains were open, and it was very light inside. There were more pictures on the walls, and a wooden case pushed up against the far wall. The top was glass, and I walked over to it and felt my blood run cold as I looked inside.

A yellowed newspaper clipping was in the direct center of the case, and the headline screamed "MURDER ON THE MOUNTAIN!"

I swallowed, and started reading.

The town of North Hollow was rocked to its very core with the discovery of the dead body of seventeen-year-old Albert Tyler. The youngster had been bludgeoned to death by what Sheriff Lincoln thinks was a shovel.

This was the first recorded murder in North Hollow since Indian times.

Young Albert had gone missing the day before. He had gone into the forest to pick blackberries and never returned. By nightfall, his father Abram had ridden down to town from Lake Thirteen Lodge to sound the alarm and organize a search party. At first it was feared he might have come across a bear or fallen and been injured. Search parties combed the woods on the side of the mountain. Young Albert had only recently graduated from North Hollow High School, and was going to be attending Columbia University in New York City this fall. Albert was a bright lad, and well liked by everyone.

He was last seen at breakfast on Monday, after which he went hunting in the woods. When he hadn't returned by lunchtime, his parents became concerned and started looking for him. Mr. Tyler tried to enlist the assistance of his hired man, Robert Shelby, but there was no sign of Shelby anywhere either—he, too, had seemingly disappeared into the woods along with young Albert. Mr. Tyler continued the search throughout the afternoon, to no avail. Once the sun came up the following morning, the search party went out looking. Later that day, a team of searchers found young Albert's slain body in the woods alongside the stream leading from Beaver Pond down to the Hudson River.

The search for Robert Shelby continues, and Sheriff Lincoln now believes that Shelby may have killed young Albert and run away. He has wired sheriffs in nearby towns to be on the alert for Shelby, that he is wanted for questioning in the murder.

There was a picture with the article, with the caption *Albert Tyler*.

It was the young man I'd seen in my visions—the one who looked so much like Marc.

I gulped and my eyes filled with tears.

"Oh, you've found the case," Miss Tyler said from behind me, startling me. I quickly wiped at my eyes as she and the others joined me.

"Miss Tyler was just telling us about the murder," Rachel said, her voice hushed. "It sounds like it was a terrible time for the town."

Miss Tyler took off her glasses and rubbed her eyes. "Uncle Albert," she said, her hands still covering her eyes. She finally looked back up at me, and her eyes were terribly sad. "My great-uncle, to be accurate. I never knew him, you know. Obviously, he'd been dead quite a while before I was born. He was actually my grandfather's younger brother." She blew out her breath in a sad sigh. "I'm the only Tyler still around, you know. The rest have all moved on, moved away. My great-grandfather built that lodge, as you know. My grandfather sold it about the time his mother died. He didn't live much longer than she did." She looked at each one of us in turn. "You know, North Hollow has been here since colonial times. It's a very old town…and in all those hundreds of years, there have only been a handful or so of murders." She tapped her fingers on the glass case. "Uncle Albert was one of them."

"Did you hear that, Scotty?" Carson's voice was hushed. *"Murdered."*

I bit my lower lip and just nodded. The sadness was filling me again, starting in my stomach, which felt knotted and sour. I couldn't speak even if I wanted to.

Poor Albert. It was Albert I was seeing in the woods, swimming in the pool. It can't be a coincidence that he looks so much like Marc. I'm going to have to tell them about it, now that they've seen his picture here. Murdered. Murdered at the cabin. No wonder it affected me so much to be there. But—

There had to be more to it than just him being murdered. Why would he care if we knew about that?

"It was a terrible, terrible tragedy," Miss Tyler went on. "My great-grandmother never got over it, and from what I heard, my great-grandfather never did, either. I don't remember ever seeing her smile, and she rarely laughed. Of course she was pretty old by the time I was born...but my father always used to tell me she was always like that, for as long as he could remember. She mourned her baby boy's murder until the day she died. He was the youngest, you know. He was her favorite."

"That's awful," Rachel whispered. "I can't even imagine."

"My great-grandfather apparently never set foot in church again—they say he cursed God—and he'd been a pillar of the church up till then, a deacon." Miss Tyler tapped the glass. "This case was my great-grandmother's. She kept all this memorabilia of his after he died. My grandfather had this case made to keep everything." She sighed. "Like I said, she never got over losing Albert the way she did." She tapped the glass again. "He was going to be the first Tyler to go to college, too—the first person from North Hollow, for that matter. Everyone in town thought a great deal of my great-uncle Albert."

I stepped away from the case and walked over to the window. I was having some trouble breathing.

"He's gorgeous," I heard Rachel say behind me. "What a good-looking young man he was."

"He went missing," she went on. "The lodge had been doing really well, so they'd hired someone to help out. They built a cabin for him to live in, a little farther down the mountain—his name was Robert Shelby. He worked for them for a couple of years, and then one summer Albert went missing." She got a faraway look in her eyes. "They found him in the woods, by the side of the creek that runs out of Beaver Pond. His head had been smashed in—they assumed he'd been hit with a shovel, and Shelby had disappeared. Everyone was shocked, and they never found Shelby. They figured he went down to New York City and just disappeared there, changed his name. No one really knew much about him to begin with, he was just a drifter who'd shown up looking for work."

But I'd seen Albert, shirtless, coming out of Shelby's cabin. Chopping wood—he seemed at *home* there.

None of this made any sense.

There's more to this story than anyone knows.

"Wow." Logan breathed. "That's—that's *awful.*"

"We don't really have anything here about the murder, of course, other than that one article there my great-grandmother kept." She sighed. "But the town library has copies of the town paper from back then, of course."

"Were there any stories in your family about…" Carson swallowed. "Anyone seeing Albert's ghost?"

I winced. I couldn't believe he asked that.

"Carson!" Rachel slapped his shoulder.

"It's a fair question." He defended himself. "Violent deaths can result in hauntings."

"Let me apologize for my brother, Miss Tyler," Rachel went on. "Ever since he interned for that crazy TV show about hauntings earlier this summer, he sees ghosts everywhere. I'm so sorry."

Instead of being offended, though, Miss Tyler threw her head back and let out a big laugh. She wiped at her eyes when she was finished. "I'm sorry, I didn't mean to laugh at you. But there's no such thing as ghosts, you know. And no one ever saw Albert after they put him in the ground. Believe me, I'd have heard about that."

We thanked her and walked out to the sidewalk. We stopped at a café a few doors down, and after we'd ordered, Carson said, "Well, there you have it. That's why Albert hasn't passed over to the other side. He was murdered, and there's something he wants us to know, and once we know what it is, he'll pass over. Maybe"—he hesitated—"maybe he can't rest because he never got justice."

"Great," Logan said with a laugh. "Unless that Shelby guy somehow managed to live to be over a hundred, I'm sure he's been dead for quite some time. So poor murdered Albert isn't getting any justice anytime soon."

"I don't know, I can't believe that Robert Shelby killed him," I said slowly. Everyone turned to look at me, and I bit my lower lip. Now was the time to tell them, at least part of it, at least the part about the guy I saw. But not that he was Albert, and not that he looked like Marc. When I was finished, Carson's face turned red.

"You can't not tell us everything you're experiencing." Carson's voice shook with anger. "That's cheating, Scotty, and—"

"It's not happening to *you*," I snapped. "And I'm really tired of everyone treating me like this is some kind of game, or I'm some kind of freak! Brain tumors and possession and ghosts!" I rubbed my eyes. I felt so tired suddenly, tired of them, tired of the situation, tired of everything. I pushed my chair back. "I'm going to go outside and make a call."

Once I was outside, I took a few deep breaths and leaned against the building. I really needed to talk to Marc.

I pulled out my phone and checked it. I had four bars, and I quickly texted: *I really miss you and want to talk to you.*

It wasn't like I could tell him what was going on. How do you put that in a text? Especially one his dad might read?

Marc didn't have a smartphone. His father didn't approve of teenagers having their own phones, in general, so both Marc and his sister had crappy, cheap pay-as-you-go cell phones, with limited data plans. Both Marc and his sister had to pay for the phones themselves, and Marc always had to be careful to make sure he conserved his minutes. The one advantage to his phone was he could receive an unlimited number of text messages, so I always texted him first and he would call me if he could. As I stood there, watching the townspeople go about their business, I closed my eyes.

"I know I keep asking, but are you okay?" Teresa asked.

I opened my eyes and smiled at her. "Yeah, sorry I was such an asshole." I swallowed. "It's just a lot to handle, you know? And all this time I thought it was *Albert* calling me. Now, I'm not so sure." I shook my head. "I don't know." I stared at my phone, scrolling through pictures. "And I really miss my boyfriend…"

"Well it's all kind of crazy, if you think about it." Teresa replied with a smile and grabbed my phone. "Wow. He's hot."

I grinned back at her and scrolled through thumbnails, then clicked on an extra-hot pic. I'd taken it at a carwash the football team had had earlier in the summer. Marc was wearing long white basketball shorts and no shirt—and someone had just sprayed him with the hose, so he was dripping wet and completely adorable.

Teresa stared at the picture before handing my phone back. "I miss my boyfriend, too." She leaned against the wall next to me. "Try not to be so hard on Carson, though. I know this whole thing is crazy, but you know he means well." She took my hand in hers. "You know we all love you, Scotty. You're family. No one gave a crap about the gay thing, but that had to be really scary for you, sending that e-mail. I don't know if I could be that brave."

"I don't know." I smiled at her. "Thanks, Teresa. I appreciate it. I suppose I should apologize to Carson." I swallowed. "This is just so weird. I—I want to believe that it's ghosts, because the alternative is that I'm going crazy. But to listen to everyone argue about what it might be, like I'm not even there—it's a bit too much to take."

"Come on," she said, pulling on my hand. "Carson really feels like crap."

I followed her back inside and sat back down at the table. Before anyone could say anything, I said, "Sorry, you guys. I shouldn't have snapped like that, but please understand—I'm scared. This is all a bit much to wrap my head around, okay?"

"I'm sorry too." Carson replied. His voice was contrite, and he wouldn't look up from his plate. "I get a little carried away because, you know, I'm excited. If this really is a haunting—"

"I'm sorry, too." Rachel cut him off. "I didn't really want it to be a brain tumor." She swallowed. "I'd rather it be a ghost, to be honest." She looked over at Carson. "And I'm sorry, Carson. I should be more supportive of your interests."

"No, no, it's okay," Carson insisted. "We always need a skeptic, someone who doesn't believe, to keep us honest."

"Oh, for Christ's sake, are we all going to sing 'Kumbaya' now?" Logan rolled his eyes.

We all laughed, the tension cut.

CHAPTER NINE

M arc never called. He didn't even text me back.

The drive back up to the lodge was pretty quiet other than the music pounding through the car stereo—Rachel, Teresa, and Carson fiddled with their phones until we passed Cemetery Road and all signals were lost. When we got back to the lodge, the parents were all sitting around, waiting for us. They'd had their lunches and didn't want to waste another minute of the trip without some family time—and the plan for the rest of the day was waterskiing. Mr. Bartlett met us down at the dock on Lake Thirteen, where the boat was tied up. After going over boat safety and making sure there were enough life preservers on board for everyone to use, he headed back up to the lodge.

We spent the entire afternoon out on the lake, waterskiing in the cold water. At first, it seemed surreal—after everything that had been going on, the normality of spending time with our parents, either piled in the boat or sitting on the dock watching, seemed strange. There was never an opportunity for us to talk about anything, as at least one parent was always around. I'd always enjoyed waterskiing, and this time was no exception. The tug on the rope pulling me up to my feet, skimming across the surface of the water at high speed, the sun on my face and the wind in my hair—when I was out on the water, I could forget everything else that was going on. I could forget about Marc not texting me back, the possibility of ghosts in the forest, a ruined cabin and seeing visions of the past when I wasn't expecting it. I was able to forget all of it, and just enjoy myself, relax and laugh and have fun with my family and my friends—the way the trip was supposed to go, the way all the ones we'd taken together in the past had gone.

It was late when we decided to quit, the sun hanging low in the western sky. But even then, we didn't get a chance to do anything, to hang out and talk and discuss what we wanted to do next, or compare notes on everything we'd found out so far. We all had dinner at the lodge, and after the dessert plates were cleared, the adults flatly refused to let us go hang out in the game room, insisting we play cards with them until my eyes were crossing from exhaustion.

I barely had the energy to undress in my room and get under the covers. I was asleep almost the moment my head hit the pillow.

And of course, I dreamed.

I was walking through the woods again, on the same path we'd followed that morning, the one that led to the cabin. I was alone as I walked this time, but I was in a really good mood—my step was light and I was grinning from ear to ear. The forest was alive with sound—the chirping of birds, the buzzing of insects, the call of wild animals rustling through the underbrush. I wasn't afraid—there was no sense of fear or danger anywhere in the woods that morning— because it was morning, a beautiful spring morning with everything blooming and the mixed scents floating gently on the warm breeze. The winter was definitely over, and now the only sign remaining of it was the sharp bite of chill I felt only when I walked through the shadows in the forest. If anything, I was excited. *I'm going to see him.* My heart was singing, and the anticipation was so much I could hardly stand it. I was whistling. I loved him and he loved me and we were going to be together, we were going to spend the entire day together, and no one would know. Everyone else was gone. We were the only two people on the mountain, which was a rare enough occasion as it was, but I was so happy and thrilled I could barely feel the ground beneath my feet as I walked, it was like I was walking on air—for that matter, I was so happy I felt like I could fly. I'd never been so in love like this before, I'd never felt so close to another person and had never thought I'd ever feel this way. I could even believe in God now, because after a lifetime of cursing him and hating him for making me the way I was, now I understood. I couldn't feel this exquisite, almost-painful joy were I not made the way God had made me, and it all made sense now, now that I had met him and had fallen in love and he loved me, too. Sure, we had to keep it all a secret from everyone else—I knew all too well how no one would understand, I had already suffered and I wasn't willing to suffer that way, ever again.

And at the end of summer we were going to go away together once and for all! No one would ever be able to keep us apart.

I had never believed I could be this happy.

I came around the corner and there was the little cliff and the roof of the cabin, which always made my heart lift a little bit every time I saw it. And there he was, my love, my true love, the man I wanted to spend the rest of my life with. He had his back to me, was swinging his ax, and the sun was shining down on his bare back, and I just stood there watching as the muscles moved underneath the skin, and then he stopped and turned and looked up at me, and his face broadened into a huge smile—

—and it was Marc, my Marc, and my heart lifted and I broke into a smile and I started running down the path, hurrying down the little footpath down to the level clearing, and he was waiting for me at the bottom and I ran into his arms and he put his arms around me and our mouths came together as he lifted me up and swung me around and I loved him so much, so very, *very* much, that my heart almost was hurting, it was so big and beating so hard against my ribs I could almost feel it and he was whispering in my ear how much he loved me and wanted me and how we were going to be together forever—

—and a cloud went over the sun and everything got dark, and I sensed it, something was watching us, and whatever it was, it hated…it hated us and wanted to destroy us…

I sat up in my bed, shivering.

The clock on the nightstand read 3:10 a.m.

And I heard it outside, the voice calling, and the heartbreak and pain and the loss, oh God, the loss, was there in the tone of his voice. It made my very soul hurt.

"Bertie…"

I wrapped my arms around my legs and shivered, it was so cold, so cold I felt like I might never be warm again. I reached over and turned on the lamp on the bedside table, flooding the room with light, and I blinked until my eyes adjusted. The air conditioner was running, and I got out of bed and ran over to it, hit the button to shut it off, and with a sigh it went off.

"Bertie…"

The sadness was so horrible to hear, the voice sounded like a sob, and I could feel it deep inside of my soul, in every part of my brain, every fiber of my very being.

The voice was calling to me.

And I wanted to go to it. The sound was pulling at me as I slipped on my shorts and the shirt I'd worn, still shivering in the cold.

And still, the voice called to me.

The pain…the pain in that voice was breaking my heart. I had to do something. I had to find the caller and put my arms around him, kiss away his tears, hold him until he realized I was there for good, we were together and would never be separated again, we were meant to be together which was why it hurt so bad…and I choked back my own sob, wiped the tears from my own eyes as I got up and walked to the back door.

I hesitated with my hand on the knob.

Maybe I shouldn't go out there I don't know who or what is calling me but it's definitely calling me it needs me and I don't sense the evil, whatever that was in the dream I felt, whatever it was I felt down at the cabin yesterday morning it can't harm me because I love him and he loves me and—

But I was still afraid.

I opened the back door, and it was pitch-black outside. There was no moon, no stars, no light, other than the yellow light on the back deck, nothing but pure black outside the slight area lit up with the bright yellow light, and I could still hear the voice calling me, from deep inside the woods.

"Bertie…Bertie…Bertie…"

Terrified as I was, I knew I couldn't just stand there listening. I took a deep breath and walked down the steps and could feel the chilly dirt beneath my bare feet and I started walking up the path, and once I stepped out of the circle of yellow light it was indeed dark, so dark I couldn't see my feet when I looked down, could barely see my hands when I held them in front of my face, it was so damned dark. And the trees were moving in the wind, rustling and seeming to whisper as branches rubbed against each other.

But I kept walking and my eyes slowly adjusted to the darkness, and I could make out the shapes of trees in the murkiness and kept walking, up the path into the woods, turning right at the fork, heading for the ruined cabin hidden so deep in the woods, away from prying eyes and away from everything and everyone.

He was waiting for me there.

"Berrrrrrrrrrrrrrrrrrrrrrrrrrr-tiiiiiiiiiiiiiieeeeeeeeeeeee."

The longing, the aching, the sadness and want and need in the voice broke my heart, and I walked faster, tears forming in my eyes and running down my cheeks, I couldn't stand it, he sounded so heartbroken and sad and lonely, and I kept going, one foot in front of the other and the woods were silent, completely silent, no birds no nothing and on I went, leaving the safety of my own cabin far behind me, and then I was there, I'd made it.

I could barely make out the ruined roof.

And I realized the voice had stopped calling.

I stood there and felt the fear start at the back of my neck, the goose bumps starting to rise, my skin crawling…There was something else there, not him, not the one I wanted, something that wanted me, wanted to do me harm, that *hated* me, hated me with such a horrible intensity that it went deep inside my soul, I'd never known that such hatred was possible but clearly it was, it wanted to kill me and destroy me because it thought I didn't deserve not only to be happy but I didn't deserve to live, and I could feel the terror I was so terrified but I couldn't move, my feet had taken root on the spot, I needed to start running, I needed to get out of there, I had to get out of there, something, *someone* was there that wanted to do me harm, who hated me so much that it was single-minded in its determination to hurt me and punish me and make me suffer it wanted to see me suffer and would laugh at my agonies and would watch as I lay dying at its feet and I was afraid so very afraid and it was there, I could see it, something dark coming down the path from the woods and it was evil and dark and it was coming for me and I opened my mouth to scream—

❖

"And that's when I woke up—and it was morning." I shivered, picking up my coffee cup and taking another big swig. Even now that it was daylight, and I was in the dining room of the lodge, with a plate full of food and my friends gathered around me, I couldn't shake the horror and terror I'd experienced. It had been so vivid, so real—even more so than the first night. The first dream had been bad enough, but to dream that I'd woken up into another nightmare? "I'm still scared, to be honest," I said, lowering my voice. "If this is the kind of dream I can expect to have every night I'm here—I don't know that I want to go bed, you know?" I speared a sausage and popped it into my mouth.

"You poor thing." Rachel shook her head, her dark hair bouncing. "You're sure it was a dream? You didn't actually go walking in the woods?"

"Well…" I closed my eyes and thought about it. "No, I'm pretty sure." I shuddered and speared another sausage. It seemed a little unreal to be sitting in the dining room, eating and talking so calmly about nightmares. I barked out a small little laugh. "I do feel like I'm going to lose my mind a bit, you know?" I tried to find the words to put it properly, to make them understand. I waved my fork with the sausage on the end. "Like this might not be real, like this is going to suddenly turn into something awful and I'm going to wake up all over again."

"I can't even begin to imagine how terrible that must be." She shivered. "I think we can all agree this is getting worse, not better." She glanced over at the table where the adults sat, laughing and joking and eating and making plans for the day. "Really, you guys. I don't think we can keep this from his parents much longer."

"She has a point, much as I hate to admit it," Logan said after swallowing a mouthful of scrambled eggs. "We're going to have to tell them at some point, and they're not going to be happy we kept this from them this long. They're going to be pissed we didn't come to them right away. You know how they are."

Teresa gave him a sour look. "They'll think we're all crazy, is what they'll think—they won't believe us for a minute, you know. They'll think we're making it all up to cover up something else. And they'll definitely punish us. And I don't know about you, dear twin, but I don't enjoy being punished."

"Albert *is* trying to tell us something, that's the reality," Carson mused before popping a piece of bacon in his mouth. "There's something he needs us to know. That's why he can't rest, and he has a connection to Scotty. Once we figure out what it is that he's trying to tell us, then he can rest and we don't have to worry about any of this—"

"I don't think Robert Shelby killed him." I glanced over at the adults' table just to reassure myself they couldn't hear anything we were saying. I took a deep breath. "That's what I think he's trying to tell me—that's why I'm seeing these things, his memories, whatever the hell it is. And I'm not convinced it's Albert that's trying to communicate with me. I mean, Albert would hardly be calling himself, would he?" I took a deep breath. It was time to come clean. "And I haven't been totally honest." I could feel my face starting to redden. "The guy I've been seeing? It's been Albert. And Albert looks like the guy I'm seeing back home."

I looked down at my plate to avoid the four pairs of eyes staring at me.

Teresa cleared her throat. "Why didn't you tell us this before?"

I didn't look up. "I don't know. I'm sorry. I guess I thought—I thought you guys might think I was making everything up or would make fun of me or think I was, I don't know, doing it for attention."

Rachel put her hand on top of mine. "Did you really think we'd stop caring about you because you're gay? Because that's crazy, Scotty. You're still Scotty."

I didn't say anything as my eyes welled up with tears. The wall inside of me shattered in that moment, and I hadn't realized until then how much I'd been holding back with all of them, how much I'd feared they'd reject me and turn their backs on me. Instead I took another sip of my coffee while I tried to get myself together.

"Of course." Carson broke the silence finally, slapping his forehead with his hand. "I'm an idiot."

"Finally he admits it." Rachel rolled her eyes. "I've been saying it for years."

He glowered at her. "We've been operating under the assumption that Albert's not at rest, that he's been trying to communicate through Scotty all this time. I based that on the fact that Albert was murdered. But the voice is calling him, isn't it? Why would the voice be calling *Albert* if Albert was the spirit trying to communicate with us?"

"Maybe there's a second ghost?" Teresa suggested.

"Great." Logan shook his head. "Like one ghost wasn't enough?"

"I don't know, but I really don't think Albert or whoever it is means any harm," I said slowly. "I don't get that sense from it, you know? All I get is sadness and loneliness. But then it turns, you know? There's that other...whatever it is, *that* seems threatening, and I never get that sense from Albert." I shook my head. "I mean, you've heard it. The voice just sounds so pathetic and sad...it just doesn't seem like it could be threatening."

"Maybe it was just a dream, Scotty," Rachel replied. "And maybe it's tricking you—luring you out with the sadness so it can get to you." She shuddered. "Ugh, sorry—what a horrible thought."

"We have to consider every possibility," Carson insisted. "We can't refuse to consider something because it's unpleasant. We can't rule out the possibility that the spirit—whatever and whoever it may be—might just want to take over Scotty's body."

And that pretty much ended the conversation.

But I knew it wasn't the case—somehow I just knew that the voice didn't really mean me any harm. Yes, it frightened me, but not because of a sense of threat, but because it was something from beyond my experience. I was also certain there *was* something out there threatening me—that sense of terror was so palpable, I couldn't be making that up—but it wasn't the voice. I just knew it.

Just like I knew it was weird that I hadn't heard from Marc.

After breakfast we were spending the day at Fort Ticonderoga, so I was hoping to have cell service for most of the day at the very least. I kept hoping Marc would call me while we were at the fort, or at least send me a text.

But he didn't. I kept starting to type out one to him at least a thousand times while we were exploring the fort but canceled them all without sending them.

I couldn't help but feel something was wrong with him.

We stopped for dinner on the way back, and darkness was already falling by the time we made it up the side of the mountain, back to the lodge. Even though it was only about ten, I was exhausted and begged off doing anything. "I can walk back by myself," I protested when my dad offered to drive me back. "And it's not that far."

"You sure you're okay?" Carson whispered.

"Seriously," I replied with a shake of my head. "I'm just tired. I didn't sleep that great last night, remember?" I lowered my voice. "I'm okay, really. I just want to go to bed."

"Okay."

"'Night, everyone," I said and walked to the end of the parking lot and started down the road. I thought about taking the shortcut through the woods, but after that dream I didn't think I wanted to be in the woods by myself. When I went around the curve and started down the mountain, I moved out of the lodge's outside light and plunged into utter darkness. The sky was full of clouds, and there was no light, no stars or moon above my head. There was nothing but inky blackness.

Just like in my dream.

I froze, unable to walk any farther.

The night was still, there was no sound anywhere other than the wind in the trees.

I no longer could hear any voices from the direction of the lodge—everyone must have gone inside.

I thought about turning around and heading back, pretending like I'd gotten a second wind rather than gotten scared...I couldn't tell the adults I'd gotten scared because they'd think I was just a baby being afraid of the dark.

"You're being stupid," I said out loud, and my voice sounded loud in the silence, loud enough to be unnerving. "You're just scaring yourself."

Calm down.

But there is something out there in the woods that wants to hurt me.

"You're being ridiculous." I took another step forward. "You're just keyed up because you haven't heard from Marc."

Maybe that was the problem, I told myself, forcing myself to start walking again. The road slanted down, and I found myself moving really quickly.

"Berrrrrrrrrrrrrrrrrrrrrrrrrrr-tiiiiiiiiiiiiieeeeeeeeeeeee."

The sound surrounded me, like it was coming from every direction, and I stifled a scream. Every hair on my body was standing up, and the Thai food I'd had for dinner was churning in my stomach. Every instinct I had told me to run as fast as I could back to the safety of the lodge, that I was crazy for trying to walk back to my cabin alone, I could always curl up and sleep on the sofa in the game room and who cared if the adults thought I was being a baby or childish or whatever, anything was better than being alone out here on the road in the dark.

"Berrrrrrrrrrrrrrrrrrrrrrrrrrr-tiiiiiiiiiiiiieeeeeeeeeeeee."

"Who—who's there?" I called out, my voice shaking almost as much as I was, repeating over and over to myself that maybe Logan or someone had come out to walk me back, not wanting me to be alone out there with whatever it was, how could I have been so stupid as to come out here alone...

I heard another sound, different from the voice, coming from the woods to my left. A twig snapped, the sound of a bush being brushed aside as someone—or something—walked past.

"Hello?"

I started walking again, my legs shaking so much that my knees almost gave with every step. I was breathing hard and fast and knew if I didn't get calm, I was going to hyperventilate. I could hear my heart pounding in my ears. My teeth were chattering, my lips trembling, and my eyes were filling with tears of sheer terror. I kept moving forward and almost sobbed in relief when I saw the yellow light from the back deck of our cabin. I half walked, half ran off the road and across the back lawn to the cabin, shakily putting my key into the lock of the door to my bedroom.

"Berrrrrrrrrrrrrrrrrrrrrrrrrr-tiiiiiiiiiiiiiiieeeeeeeeeeeee."

Now, in the light, I wasn't as frightened as I had been in the darkness.

I closed my eyes and pushed the fear aside, and opened my mind.

There was a weird feeling of exaltation for just a moment, and then it was like I was being filled up on the inside, my mind was being pushed aside as something else was getting inside of me, inside my head and my mind.

I fell back against the door and slid down to the deck.

And the darkness faded...and it was daylight again.

I got to my feet and walked down the steps to the path. The sun was out, was high, it was close to noon, and I started walking, my underarms sweating. I wasn't wearing a shirt, it was tossed over my one shoulder, and I was hungry, really hungry, and I wanted to get back to the cabin—

—I didn't want to eat with the family up at the lodge, I didn't feel quite so safe there as I used to or as welcomed, Mrs. Tyler of course hadn't changed, she was just as friendly and nice as she always was, always doing her best to make me feel like I was a part of the family, but I had some fresh bread there and some chicken in the icebox, I was going to need to get more ice the next time I went down into town, best not to forget or everything would spoil, and I kept walking and I was happy, so I started whistling as I walked, it was a gorgeous day and blessed was I to be alive on such a gorgeous day, I had my health and I was young and strong and lucky, very lucky because I'd found love even if it was the wrong kind of love, the kind of love that had gotten me run out of Boston, but how could love be wrong, love was a sign of favor from God, wasn't it, and then I came around the curve in the path and he was down there, I could see him chopping wood, his broad strong back muscles flexing and moving as he swung the ax, and my heart swelled with so much love it felt like it could almost burst and then—

—and I opened my eyes and I was back in the forest, and it was night again, it was pitch-black and I felt terror, absolute stark raving terror because I didn't know how I'd gotten there, and there was something out there in the darkness, and it wanted me, I could feel the hate and cold emanating from it, *hatred,* it wanted to destroy me and kill me, and I stifled a scream and turned to run back up the path.

But I stumbled, tripping on a root or something, and I let out a half cry as I fell, hitting the ground so hard that the breath was knocked out of me and my head struck something hard and stars danced in front of my eyes and I could hear it over my labored breathing, I couldn't catch my breath but whatever it was it was coming, it was coming for me and it was cold and evil and it wanted to kill me, and I got to my hands and knees and started scrambling for safety, absolutely terrified it was going to get me, whatever it was wanted me dead, it hated me with an intensity I could feel, and then I could breathe again and I was standing straight up and running, and the tears were running down my face and I was sobbing, sobbing with sadness and fear and terror, absolute terror, and it was going to get me, I wasn't going to get away...

"Berrrrrrrrrrrrrrrrrrrrrrrrrrrr-tiiiiiiiiiiiiiiieeeeeeeeeeeeee."

And I heard the voice, echoing through the trees sadly, that hollow sorrow filling me and surrounding me, and suddenly I could see the yellow light again, and the voice kept calling.

"Berrrrrrrrrrrrrrrrrrrrrrrrrrrr-tiiiiiiiiiiiiiiieeeeeeeeeeeeee."

And I stumbled out of the woods and across the lawn, made it up the steps and collapsed, sobbing and breathing hard, on the deck. And the sense of evil wasn't there anymore, I'd managed to somehow get away from it, and I was safe.

For now.

The keys were still dangling in the deadbolt, and somehow I managed to get the deadbolt turned, and I stumbled inside, slamming the door shut and locking it behind me.

I staggered into the bathroom and splashed cold water on my face.

My eyes were wide open and bloodshot, my skin so pale it was almost bluish.

I filled up a glass with cold water and gulped it down.

My hands shaking slightly, I brushed my teeth and washed my face again.

I walked back out into the bedroom.

The dark was out there, outside the windows.

I walked around, pulling down blinds and closing curtains.

I didn't want to know what was out there, if anything.

I sat down on the bed and covered my face in my hands.

Maybe Rachel was right. Maybe I was losing my mind.

But I was willing to swear on a stack of Bibles that just minutes ago it had been broad daylight in the woods.

What was going on? What was happening to me?

Remembering what Carson had said, I got out my iPad, opened a note, and with trembling fingers started typing out what had just happened to me.

When I was finished, I saved it and closed my tablet, putting it down on the nightstand. I slowly got undressed and got under the covers.

I didn't turn out the light—I didn't want to let the dark into the bedroom with me.

I knew it was crazy but didn't care.

And, somehow, I managed to fall asleep.

CHAPTER TEN

"Maybe I am losing my mind." I laughed bitterly. "Anything would be better than this."

We were all sitting on the porch of the lodge after breakfast the next morning. Somehow I'd managed to get some sleep, even though it seemed like I kept waking up every five minutes. Even when I was asleep, it was that horrible half sleep where I felt like all I had to do was open my eyes and I'd be awake. When I heard my mother moving around in the kitchenette, I'd finally given up and gotten out of bed. I'd had two cups of coffee with her before grabbing my iPad and heading up to the lodge. I'd deliberately taken the shortcut through the woods, just to see if anything would happen.

Nothing did, of course.

I let everyone read my write-up of what I'd experienced last night while we had breakfast, and once we were finished we moved outside to the porch. Our parents had set off for the lake to go kayaking—when asked to join them, we'd all said no because we wanted to go hiking in the woods. That was the cover story Carson had come up with.

The truth was, Carson wanted to go look for the place where Albert's body had been found over a hundred years earlier. I wasn't so certain it was a great idea, myself, but I also didn't want to look like I was a coward—and there would be safety in numbers, I figured.

"I don't think so," Carson replied, scratching his chin. "For one thing, people who are losing their minds generally don't think they are, you know. They think they're completely sane. And you keep forgetting—we've all heard the voice calling. If not for that, yeah, I'd say it was a much greater possibility. And I really don't think it's a collective hallucination." He smiled at me, flipping my iPad closed and handing it back over to me. "I also don't think there's a more logical explanation for what's happening. We've pretty much ruled everything out except the supernatural."

"Besides, if you were actually going crazy, you'd have been experiencing it before you got here," Rachel went on. "And there wasn't anything, was there? You weren't seeing or hearing things at home you haven't told us about, were you?"

"No." I shook my head. "Everything at home was normal. The summer was almost ridiculously boring, to be honest. The only thing that changed was—well, you know what changed." In the distance, I could see our parents on the dock, putting the kayaks into the lake. I sighed and leaned against the rough-hewn railing. "And being gay isn't a mental illness."

"No one said it was," Teresa replied, frowning. "You keep acting like we're homophobic or something, Scotty. It's irritating and it's unfair and it's not true." She folded her arms. "We're not, so get over yourself, okay? And it's not like that's going to help us figure out what's going on with you."

"Exactly," Logan chimed in, a scowl on his face. "It's almost like you're doing it for attention."

"What? I'm sorry—that's not what I meant, really. I was just saying…" I couldn't believe what I was hearing. I looked at Logan, who had the decency to blush and look away. Carson was staring at his hands, Rachel was fiddling with her phone, and only Teresa was looking right at me. "Is that what you all think? That I'm doing this for attention?" My head was spinning and the eggs and sausage I'd had for breakfast were churning in my stomach. "Wow. Just wow."

My eyes filled with tears. *Wow,* I thought, getting up out of my chair and blindly walking off the porch, heading down the long lawn in the direction of the lake. I heard Teresa call my name but I ignored her. Fuck her, fuck all of them. I didn't bother trying to stop the tears, letting them run down my face. *I am sooooo sorry to have disrupted your vacation with my stupidity and my self-absorption and my problems. Well fuck every last one of you, I don't need you, I don't need anyone and I won't interfere with your precious vacation any more, okay?*

I could see the three kayaks making their way out away from the shore as I walked. I felt hurt, angry, betrayed. My phone started buzzing in my pocket as I got closer to the dock. My hands were shaking so hard I almost dropped it when I pulled it out of my shorts pocket. I stopped walking and ran my finger across the screen to unlock it.

And there it was, a text from Marc. Dated last night.

Sorry man dad took our phones things have been crazy lately miss you marc.

I was so relieved I didn't stop myself from sitting down hard in the grass as my knees buckled. *Thank you, God,* I thought as I reread the message over and over again. I hadn't realized until then just how worried about him I'd been.

I wiped at my eyes and took a deep breath.

Maybe they're right. Maybe I'm just being a big old drama queen and all of this was triggered out of my worry about Marc?

But that didn't make any sense.

I didn't want to risk moving and losing the cell signal, so I touched the screen to reply and typed quickly *hope everything is okay I miss you be home on Sunday hang in there buddy.*

I hated that I couldn't say that I loved him, that I wanted to kiss him and hug him, tell him how lonely I was without being able to see his face and his adorable smile every day.

But if his father saw it…I didn't even want to think about what that would trigger in his dad. I looked out at the lake and saw my parents paddling their kayak, perfectly in sync.

I'm so lucky I have the parents I do, I thought. *So very, very lucky.*

I touched the little send button, and my phone made the whooshing sound that meant the message had been sent.

"Hey, Scotty, I'm sorry," Teresa said as she sat down next to me. "Logan shouldn't have said that, and I sure as hell didn't mean to hurt your feelings." Tentatively, she put her arm around my shoulders. "I love you—we all do, Scotty. We're like family." She squeezed me, and I put my head down on her shoulder, resisting the urge to just start bawling my head off. "We're all worried about you, you know. Not because you're gay, but…" Her voice trailed off for a moment. "There's so much hatred out there for gays, Scotty. And all this crazy shit that's been happening ever since we got here…" She swallowed. "My first thought when you told me was…you know, about the bullying and everything…"

"It's okay, Teresa, I overreacted, I'm kind of all wound up," I replied, pulling up a few blades of grass and tossing them up in the air. The wind caught them and carried them away. "Logan was just being honest—and I haven't been. I should have told you guys that Albert looked like Marc. I should have told you guys about the emotions I experienced whenever I was seeing whatever it was Albert wanted me to see. I just was afraid, you know? I was afraid you guys would think I was making it all up."

"That Albert was gay?" she said quietly. "I kind of figured that out, from when you told us."

"That's just it, I don't know that Albert *was* gay." I sighed. "I'm *seeing* Albert, and you know, when I see him, I have all of these feelings—not just love but the sadness, and then the fear sometimes, too. I don't know, Teresa."

"Tell me about Marc," she said, squeezing me again. "How long have you been seeing him?"

"It's been about a year—actually, we had our first kiss the night we got back from Sanibel last year." I grinned. "I've had a crush on him since I first met him, but I never dreamed…I never thought I'd be lucky enough to have him like me back, you know?" I looked at my phone and smiled at the message again. "I heard from him finally—he texted me last night, and I just got it. He's okay." I sat there for a moment, staring at the message.

"He really does look like Albert—it's uncanny," she said, pulling out her phone and fiddling with it for a moment. She used her fingers to expand an image of Albert. She put hers down and took mine, doing the same thing to the picture of Marc until his face filled the screen of my phone. She put the two phones next to each other and smiled at them, satisfied. "It really is uncanny," she said, turning the phones to me so I could see them. "I took a picture of the article in the case at the historical society yesterday, in case we want to read it again," she explained.

"That was smart," I said as I stared at the two phones. The picture of Marc had started to blur a bit as she'd made it larger so she could get a close-up of the face, but it was clear enough. The brown sepia photograph she'd expanded on her own phone was clearer, but the resemblance was uncanny. There were, of course, slight differences—Albert looked rather glum in his photo, so I couldn't tell if he had dimples like Marc's, and his lips seemed a little thinner. The hair was different, obviously—Marc wore his cut pretty short—and Marc's face seemed a little more fleshed out than Albert's. They could have been twins. "It's pretty spooky," I said, unable to take my eyes away from the pictures on the two screens. "Albert looks more like Marc than his own sister does."

"I wonder…" She cut herself off and took her phone back from me.

"What?"

She shook her head and laughed. "I don't know—I kind of have a theory, but I don't know if I want to say anything until I've looked some more stuff up." She looked out at the lake. "I read this book—it was fiction, but the story is kind of similar to what's going on here. And with the pictures…" She shrugged. "I don't think I'll say anything until I know more, you know? There's more than enough crazy theories floating around."

"To say the least," I replied. "I know I shouldn't have lost it up there, but it's a bit much. And I don't mean what Logan said, either. This whole thing." I bit my lower lip. "It's a bit much to take to begin with, and everyone's being cool for the most part, but it would be nice if Carson didn't keep forgetting that I'm a person, not just some experiment for that stupid TV show."

"He doesn't mean anything by it, though. He's concerned for you, like we all are." She lightly kissed my cheek. "We're all scared, Scotty, and it's not really happening to us. I can't imagine how scared you must be."

I smiled at her. "I love you, Teresa."

"We'll get this all figured out." She laughed. "And even if we don't—we're only going to be here until the weekend. I'm pretty sure Albert's ghost can't follow you back to Chicago."

I laughed and looked down at the lake. I could hardly see the kayaks—they were almost to the far side of Lake Thirteen. "I sure hope not," I replied. "I don't want to share Marc with anyone."

We both laughed, and I closed my eyes and thought back, trying to remember all the times I'd seen Albert—swinging the ax, swimming in the stream farther down the mountain, the emotions I'd felt.

"And for the record, Logan was way out of line," she said gently. "There's no way you could have fixed things so that there would be these pictures of Albert looking like Marc's twin, or like he could be Marc's brother. Logan was being a dickhead, and when we get back up to the lodge I'm sure he'll apologize." She patted my leg. "And don't you think they're all going to freak out just a little bit when they see how much Albert and Marc look alike?" She stood up and brushed off the back of her shorts. She smiled at me as I stood up and hooked her arm through mine. "So, tell me more about Marc."

As we walked up the slanted lawn back to the porch, I told her everything—about how Marc and I first met, how we became friends, when I first realized I was attracted to him, how our first kiss came about.

"His dad sounds awful," she commented as we went up the three steps to the porch.

"You have no idea," I said, rolling my eyes "Hey, everybody." I gave them a feeble smile. "Sorry I got so mad. I know you're all trying to help and—"

"Dude, I'm sorry," Logan said quickly. He grabbed my hand and shook it, hard, before pulling me into a hug. "I—"

"Don't worry about it." I cut him off, extricating myself from his bear hug. Logan had no idea how strong he was, really—he'd been squeezing me so hard I could barely breathe.

"Guys, check this out." Teresa put her hand out for my phone, and I handed it to her. I wandered inside while she showed them the two pictures, getting a Coke out of the cooler. When I walked back out, Rachel was holding both phones, staring at them in disbelief.

"I'm beginning to think there's more to this than just a haunting," Carson mused. "The resemblance is really amazing. I wonder..." his voice trailed off.

"What?" Rachel demanded.

"I wonder if we found a picture of Robert Shelby—surely we'll be able to find one..." He got up and walked over to the railing. "Does anyone—would anyone rather drive into town than go out in the woods? I'm thinking we can accomplish more if we split up."

"I'll go into town," Rachel said quickly. She made a face. "I got eaten up by mosquitoes the last time, I'm not looking forward to that happening again. And, you know, snakes." She shuddered.

"I'll go with her," Teresa said. "I'm not big on snakes, either. I'm sure there's something you want us to look for in town. Maybe a picture of Robert Shelby?"

"I want you to go to the library and look up all the articles about the murder," Carson directed. "I especially want to see if you can find any pictures of him—let's hope we get lucky and there are some. But having your picture taken back then wasn't as commonplace as it is today—not everyone had cameras back then. But also see what else you can find out—if they ever found Shelby, anything you can about the Tyler family."

"All right. Miss Tyler said the library had an archive of the newspaper, which is probably the only record we'll be able to find. I'll see if they have a copy of that book about the murder, too," Teresa said, and Logan handed her the car keys. She looked at Rachel. "You ready?"

Rachel got up with a nod. "Yeah. You guys be careful, okay? Don't do anything stupid." The two of them disappeared around the side of the lodge. A few moments later, there was the sound of a car's engine starting, and then we saw the SUV heading down the road in the direction of town.

"I talked to Annie about how to find the creek," Logan said. He still seemed a little subdued, so I smiled at him. "She said the easiest thing to do is find Beaver Pond, and it's on the far side." He swallowed. "And you find Beaver Pond by following the trail past the wrecked cabin. She said there are signs farther along the path, the deeper you get into the woods." He pulled a compass out of his pocket. "And she gave me this, just in case we get lost."

"As long as we stay on the path," Carson said, "I don't see how we can get lost. But better to be safe than sorry, of course. Let's get some water and head out."

"Okay, then." Carson handed me back my phone. "What are we waiting for?"

Once we'd gotten some bottles of water out of the cooler in the lodge, we headed out across the parking lot and into the woods. Logan walked in front, and Carson walked behind me. I smiled to myself. It was obvious what they were doing—they had me surrounded in case something happened, if I had another vision or whatever it was happened to me when I was in the woods. We took the fork to the right and started heading down the side of the mountain. Once the roof of the ruined cabin came into sight, Logan started walking faster, as though he wanted to get past there as quickly as possible. That was fine with me, but I still glanced over at the wrecked building, the pile of debris on top of the covered well.

But I didn't feel anything and so kept walking, trying to keep up with Logan and his long legs. Once we were past the clearing and back into the tangle of woods again, I realized I'd been holding my breath. I let it out in a big exhale of relief. We kept having to climb over fallen trees, sometimes pushing aside brush and bushes that had overgrown the path, stepping over tiny little streams of water meandering through the forest. The ground was damp in a lot of places, and even muddy in others. Every so often the sun would break through a hole in the trees overhead, but it was cool in the woods. I was starting to breathe a little harder but wasn't feeling damp or sweaty.

And then Logan stopped walking. When I caught up to him, I saw we'd reached another fork in the path. There was a weathered old sign pointing to the left with *Beaver Pond* carved into it. Another underneath it, pointing to the right, said *Ski Trail 3*.

"I could stand to see some beaver," Logan joked, only to get a glare from Carson and an eye roll from me.

"Things not working out with Annie?" I couldn't help myself.

"Week's not over yet," he replied, digging his elbow into my ribs. "Plenty of time left for her to understand the magic that's Logan Stark."

"Magic?" Carson shook his head. "I don't know that's what it should be called."

"Black magic is magic," I pointed out, earning a good-natured laugh from Logan and a grin from Carson.

"All right, guys, let's move out," Logan said and headed down the path to the left.

We walked on in silence, with me taking pictures from time to time with my phone. If not for the path, you'd never know any humans had ever been through this part of the woods before. Logan got pretty far ahead of Carson and me, partly because he wasn't taking pictures and partly because he had longer legs and walked faster than we did, but he never quite got out of our sight.

Then he shouted, and we hurried to catch up to him.

We came out of the woods and stood next to him, looking out over a vast expanse of what appeared to be an open field, but it seemed to be overgrown with reeds and tall grasses.

"This doesn't look like a pond," Carson frowned.

"They're having a drought this year," Logan said. "So the water levels are low. Come on, she said the creek drains out of the pond on the other side." He started making his way along the lip of a ridge overlooking the meadow. I made my way after him, with Carson behind me, careful when moving branches out of the way to hold them so they didn't slap back into Carson—tempting though it was. It was beautiful out here, and I took a swig from my Coke as I maneuvered around trees and bushes. In some places, the ground was moist, and every so often I would see a break in the thick reeds where a clear stream was meandering. The sky was blue, with no clouds anywhere to be seen. I kept moving, watching a hawk soaring over the meadow. It seemed like we were walking forever, and it also seemed to me that there had to be a path somewhere away from the bank of this so-called pond that would be easier to traverse—but as we moved around, I could see a cement wall in the distance running from a ridge on the same side of the meadow we were on to another ridge. I pointed it out to Logan.

"Someone built that to manage floods, I guess," he said. "I imagine when the snows melt up here there's a lot of runoff."

And the moment he finished speaking I could see it: all the trees bare of leaves, snow covering the ground, the meadow itself an expansive sheet of gray ice with piles of snow here and there. It made me shiver.

"You okay?" Logan looked at me with an odd expression on his face.

"I'm good," I said and started walking again.

About ten minutes later, the reeds finally gave way to the surface of the pond. Logan was just standing there, looking out over it. He smiled at us when we caught up to him. "And there's the water." He pointed to the cement wall, which was clearly a dam. "My guess is the creek is on the other side of the dam." He grinned.

"I would have thought Beaver Pond meant a pond formed by a *beaver* dam," I said, a little disappointed, but I couldn't resist adding, "Looks like there's no beaver for you, Logan."

"Just my luck," he replied with a good-natured smile.

"Well, maybe they built the cement dam where a beaver dam used to be," Carson suggested.

"All right, guys, what are we waiting for?" Logan waved us on. "Let's go."

He hurried around the edge, fighting his way past bushes and low-hanging branches while Carson and I tried to keep up. He finally reached the dam, which was high over his head. He walked to the right, heading up the slope with us right behind him. About ten yards from the shoreline, the side of the slope met the top of the cement dam, and he climbed up. The top was about a yard wide, and with a whoop that echoed through the woods, he made his way out to the center.

I climbed up and gave Carson my hand to help him keep his balance as he climbed up on top. I could hear the sound of running water but couldn't see the actual stream through the trees and because of the way the hill sloped. I followed Logan out to the center and kept looking off to the right. And there it was. The clear running stream that made its way down the side of the mountain to drain into the Hudson River, the place where they'd found Albert's murdered corpse over a hundred years earlier.

"If I finished this Coke and tossed the bottle in there, it might wind up in New York Harbor," I observed, taking another drink out of it.

The creek was actually pretty narrow, with mossy stones lining the bank. There was a waterline about five feet higher on the banks. The water flowing through the bottom of the cement dam was pretty clear. I could see the bottom—it was no more than a foot or two deep at most, and schools of minnows were darting around just below the surface. Just like at the cabin, there were some rusted beer cans and other human debris scattered around along the banks, so it was probably a place for kids to come hang out and party.

We climbed down and made our way along the soggy bank. Several times I had to grab onto a branch or something as the bank crumbled beneath my sneakers.

Up ahead I could see where a tree, now covered with moss, had fallen across the creek, and—

—I was running, absolutely terrified, through the woods. He was behind me and he wanted me dead, there was no question about that, he was going to kill me. I had to keep running, I had to keep going, I had to get away. I knew the woods better than he did, that I knew—he never really came down this way, following the creek from the pond down to the river. I knew if I could just make it down to the river—if I could just get there—he wouldn't be able to do it, he wouldn't be able to kill me, not in front of everyone in the town, there simply wasn't any way he could do it. He could scream his insane accusations to everyone but they wouldn't—they *wouldn't*—believe him, and even if they did…

He was dead. A sob rose in my throat but I couldn't let that stop me, I couldn't, I had to keep going even though my heart had been ripped right out of my chest. I had to hang on to the hatred, yes, that was what I had to hold on to, that would keep me going. I couldn't do anything to stop him, of course, there was nothing I could do to stop him. My poor Bertie, my God, my God, my poor Bertie was dead...

No, no, you can't think that way focus on the *hate* you feel, you can't let him get away with it he would never know, you have to get away, you have to, people have to know what he did no matter why he did it murder is murder and they will *hang* him and Bertie poor Bertie you have to stay alive, you have to stay alive so you can tell the truth, so you can tell the sheriff what happened back there at the cabin...

And then I stumbled over a root and fell, down into the dirt and the mud right there on the bank of the stream, and as I tried to get up my ankle wouldn't hold me, my ankle hurt so badly and I knew then I was going to die...

"Right here," I said, my voice shaking somewhat. I was trembling, and my entire body was cold. "It happened right here, he died *right here.*"

Carson turned and looked back at me.

And a cloud seemed to come over the sky.

The temperature seemed to drop.

Everything was going dark.

A scream rose in my throat and I fought it down.

"Oh my God," I heard Logan whisper beside me.

And then I heard it, too—the sound of someone, *something,* crashing through the woods toward us.

Just like in my dream or vision or whatever it was I just had.

Carson's face turned completely pale. "Come on—this way! I found the path!"

And I could feel the coldness coming through the woods toward where we were standing, and I could feel the hatred.

Whatever it was, it wanted me. And it wanted me dead.

"Come on!" Logan screamed and grabbed my hand so hard I cried out. He yanked me along behind him so hard my shoulder felt like it almost pulled out of the socket, and ahead of me, I could see Carson running as fast as he possibly could.

And we followed.

The coldness, the evil that was emanating from behind us terrified me more than anything I'd ever felt in my life, it had felt like it was sucking my soul out of my body.

I ran. Logan let go of my hand at some point and took off, passing Carson as we ran on the path as it twisted and turned through the woods away from the pond and the stream. I lost or threw away my Coke at some point but I didn't care, all I cared about was getting out of the woods, getting as far away from that place as I possibly could.

My breath was coming in stitches, but I could hear Carson's labored breathing behind me as we kept going.

And, finally, we crashed through the underbrush out onto the mountain road. Logan was already there, bent double, sucking in huge gasps of air.

I tried to catch my breath and realized tears were running down the sides of my face.

"What—what the hell was that?" Logan finally managed to get the words out.

"I—I don't know." I said. My leg muscles were tying up from the running, and I paced a bit to keep them from cramping. Carson was still trying to catch his own breath, sweat running down his face, his hair completely wet.

But he was grinning at me.

"Why are you smiling?" I demanded.

"Don't you see?" He beamed at me, practically bouncing up and down on the balls of his feet with excitement. "This time it wasn't just you! *We all felt it.*"

CHAPTER ELEVEN

Once we were out of the woods and calming ourselves down, Carson quickly insisted that we not discuss what had just happened. "We can't taint each other by talking about it," he insisted. "We have to write down our independent observations and thoughts without talking."

So we walked back up the mountain road—we'd come out well below my cabin—in utter silence. Once we made it to the lodge, we all took turns at the computer in the game room. Carson had Logan go first, and while he was typing, I pulled out my phone to see if Marc had responded to my last text. There was nothing, so I checked my e-mail too. Nothing interesting, just some stuff from my high school and some of my other friends, nothing that looked important enough to download. When Logan pushed his chair back and the printer started spewing out his pages, Carson said, "Were you thorough?"

Logan rolled his eyes. "I wrote down everything I remember," he insisted. "Can I go find Annie now?"

Carson made a face and dismissed him. He gestured to the computer. "Your turn."

I put my phone away and sat down at the computer. It was an ancient Dell, so old that it was still on Windows XP. I sighed and opened a new Word document. I closed my eyes and tried to remember everything and started typing without opening my eyes. I really didn't want to relive the terror, to be honest, but I knew it was a necessary evil. I typed, my fingers flying over the keyboard, my eyes closed as I tried to remember every moment, every emotion and feeling I'd had. As the document filled with words, my fingers began to tremble a little.

I don't think I'd ever been so terrified in my life.

And it was an experience I'd be happy to go the rest of my life without having again.

When I finished, I hit the print button and deleted my document. I got up so Carson could have a seat and walked over to the window. I looked out at the lake, shining silver in the afternoon sun. Everything seemed so normal now. It was hard to believe not even an hour before we were running headlong through the woods, terrified for our lives. If this didn't come to an end soon...no matter what Teresa thought, I didn't think I could make it to the weekend without losing my mind for real if we didn't figure out how to stop this by then.

I walked back over to the printer. Carson was scowling at the computer screen and deleted an entire paragraph, starting over again while I got all the pages off the printer tray. I sat down on the L-shaped couch with my back to the window and started reading Logan's account.

Everything was fine, he'd written. *We found Beaver Pond and the little creek running out of it relatively easily. It wasn't until we started walking along the creek bank to where that newspaper story said they found Albert's body that things started to feel wrong. If I'm being honest I have to say I don't know what I was thinking about all of this before today. Scotty doesn't lie so I have to believe him unless he's changed into a different person than the Scotty I've known all my life but I don't know if I believe in ghosts or any of the stuff Carson always talks about. So anyway we were walking along the bank and it was sunny and there weren't any clouds in the sky and the next thing I know it's getting dark like the sun's gone away and I felt scared. I don't know why, I just did, I felt like I wanted to scream and just get the hell out of there as fast as I could go. But then we heard it—there was something in the woods, something we couldn't see and it was evil, and it wanted to kill all of us. I've never been so scared in my life and I hope I'm never that scared ever again and I could see something through the bushes it was black and dark and shapeless but it was there I wasn't imagining it and then Carson started running and me and Scotty ran right after him and we didn't stop running until we'd gotten all the way out of the woods and then I felt like I wasn't scared anymore because we'd gotten away from whatever that was but I don't want to go back into the woods ever.*

Reading Logan's take–brief as it was—was bad enough; I was glad he hadn't gone into as much detail as I had. I put the pages down on the coffee table and pulled out my phone again. Nothing still…I started to write another text to him but didn't really know what to say besides what I'd already said in the text he hadn't answered. And I wasn't even sure texting worked here in the game room, with no cell service. I'd hoped maybe he'd send me an e-mail…

Honestly, I was a little worried about Marc.

His dad was kind of a jerk about the phone, but he rarely limited Marc's time online with his laptop. Marc was always cautious—his dad didn't seem to be too good with technology, but Marc wasn't willing to take that chance. He always deleted my e-mails and deleted the ones he sent to me from his sent-mail folder, just to be on the safe side. I wished things could be different—I was pretty sure Mrs. Krueger would just want Marc to be happy, no matter what—but Mr. Krueger? I could only imagine how he would react. So we always, *always* had to be careful.

As long as I lived, I would never forget hearing Mr. Krueger ranting about the perverts and the faggots who were so unnatural and how giving them rights was no different than letting people marry more than one spouse or marry their dog or a horse or have sex with children. Listening to that rant had nauseated me, made me sick to my stomach.

The thought of what he might do if he ever caught Marc and me together…

That was why Marc came over to my house most of the time. We hardly ever went to his house since we got together. We could steal kisses and hugs and talk about the possibility of a future together. Of course, once my parents knew we were in love we had to leave my bedroom door open—which I always thought was silly given we'd been able to keep it closed for almost a year before they knew we were more than friends…but I guess it made them feel better in some way, and they still let him spend the night in the guest room. We obeyed their rules—we'd never had sex, just kissed and messed around a little, nothing serious or anything for them to be worried about—but since they were so cool about us, I didn't really want to push my luck with them.

Any time they made a rule or laid down the law, all I had to do was remind myself that I was lucky they weren't like the Kruegers.

I missed him so much—I hated not being able to talk to him whenever I wanted to or walk down the street and see him. We'd spent so much time together all summer—being separated like this was almost like losing a limb. Knowing that he could have been Albert Tyler's twin brother was seriously disturbing. I didn't know what that meant or even how it was possible. Maybe one of the Tylers had somehow married into either the Krueger family, or his mother's—maybe I should ask Miss Tyler at the Historical Society about it. Stranger things than that have happened, and if the Tylers had scattered all over the country the way she said they had…it was possible, wasn't it?

I heard the printer start up again and looked up to see Carson stand up and stretch. He walked over and picked up the pages I'd discarded, plopped down, and started reading. When he finished, he grinned at me. "The girls are going to freak the hell out when they read these." He held his out to me. "You want to read mine?"

I shook my head. "Logan's was so similar to mine…you can just tell me about yours."

His grin got bigger. "My experience was very similar to you two's. That growing sense of unease that turned into terror—the sounds in the woods, the darkness…and we independently corroborated each other, which makes it more scientific. I have a theory…"

Of course he had a theory. He *always* had a theory.

"So, what do you think?" I asked, slipping my phone back into the pocket of my cargo shorts.

"The good news is I think we can conclusively say you aren't going crazy." His grin got so wide it looked like his head might flip over backward. "We can definitely rule out collective hallucinations, too. That is not what just happened to us out in the woods." He shuffled the papers a bit, scowling down at them. "I wonder how much longer the girls will be?" He glanced at the clock on the wall. "I hope they didn't decide to have lunch in town." He frowned and fidgeted a bit. "I have a theory, but I want to see what the girls found—to kind of confirm what I'm thinking. And that way I only have to explain it once."

"Great," I replied, trying to keep my growing irritation out of my voice. Carson was Carson, and nothing was going to change that—ever. He'd always been that way, even when he was a little kid—he couldn't be rushed, no way. He wouldn't say or do anything until he was good and ready. It was kind of annoying, to be honest, but I guess I couldn't blame him for not wanting to have to explain it twice.

And, besides, I was curious as to what the girls might have found at the library.

I got up and walked over to the window. The adults were getting out of the lake with the kayaks. I didn't know what they had planned for the rest of the day—there'd been talk over breakfast about a trip to a garnet mine on the other side of the mountain—but I was planning on begging off from whatever it was.

The last thing I wanted to do was go exploring a mine.

I'd just sat back down on the couch when Teresa and Rachel burst into the game room, their faces lit up with excitement and something else I couldn't quite put my finger on. "Where's Logan?" Teresa demanded, tossing her enormous shoulder bag onto the coffee table before collapsing onto the couch. "You wouldn't believe what we found at the library!" She looked from me to Carson and back again. "You two look odd, what's happened? Did we miss something? Did something happen in the woods?"

Rachel rolled her eyes and barked out a sour laugh. "*Of course* something happened in the woods, Teresa. Why else would Carson look like he's going to explode and Scotty like he's had the worst morning ever?" She folded her arms and gave me a smug look. "But wait till we tell you what we found out." She bridled a little bit, looking very self-satisfied.

"So, what did you guys find out?" I asked, looking from one to the other and back again. "Something that's got you all excited, I see."

"You're not going to believe it when we tell you," Rachel replied slyly. "If I hadn't seen it for myself, I wouldn't have believed it." She gave me a real smile this time. "But what we found out—we think we've solved the entire mystery of Lake Thirteen."

"In that case, I'm going to go see if I can find Logan," I said, standing up, smiling back at her. "So we can compare notes. The sooner this is over, the better."

I checked my phone one last time and walked out of the game room into the big open space of the lodge's main room. I could hear the laughter of the adults as they came up the lawn with the kayaks, and I hurried out the front door—I didn't want to run into them yet.

I stood in the parking lot and looked around. I didn't see him anywhere. I was about to turn around and walk into the kitchen, see if maybe Annie was there or her parents knew where they'd gone...

But somehow, I just knew where they were.

On the other side of the parking lot there was an enormous shed where all the sports equipment was kept. The shed door was open, and I could see the mountain bikes chained up inside.

I walked over to it and around to the back side.

Sure enough, Logan and Annie were standing next to the shed where the equipment was kept, and as I came around the corner of the building they kissed—

—and everything changed.

The shed was still there, but it was different—it was rough-hewn wood, unsanded and unpainted. It was also a lot smaller than it had been, but I knew I was seeing into a different time yet again. I heard a horse whinny inside—of course, back then it would have been used as a stable. A boy and a girl pressed up against the back side of the stable, but it wasn't Logan and Annie I could see kissing there. I recognized the young man. The girl was wearing a long dress, her hair tied back with a ribbon, and I felt a surge of anger, pure jealousy. She pushed herself away from him and giggled before running away around the other side. I had no idea who she was, but I knew full well who the young man was.

It was Albert, and he was looking at me, his eyes sad.

"You weren't supposed to see that," he said, stepping toward me.

That was when I realized he could see me. I wasn't just observing, like I had all the times before—this time, I was a part of it.

And then it was gone like it had never happened.

I leaned back against the shed, making a loud noise. I wasn't paying any attention to Logan and Annie, my mind was caught up in what I'd just seen.

I wasn't Albert. I wasn't seeing through Albert's eyes.

Then whose?

I'd kind of known all along—I was getting flashes of memory, whatever the spirit could send to me, as it tried to tell me what had happened in 1907.

Annie pushed Logan away and ran off around the side of the lodge, leaving him standing there staring after her with a stunned look on his face. "Nice going," he snarled at me. "Haven't you ever heard of being discreet?"

I shook my head and took a few deep breaths. "The girls are back," I said after a few moments. His face was flushed, and he was angry. I couldn't make myself care. It didn't matter. "Sorry," I said, "but we need to get back to the game room. You can make out with Annie later."

"Yeah, I heard them drive up," he said, still staring off in the direction Annie had run. He gave me a weird look and finally said, "Come on, then. Let's get this over with." But as he started to walk away, he stopped and turned back, peering at me. "Something just happened, didn't it?"

I nodded.

"You want to talk about it? Did you see something?"

"I—I don't think it's Albert—"

The adults came around the side of the building with the kayaks, drenched in sweat and looking really happy. "Hey guys," my dad called. "Once we get cleaned up, we're going to head into town for lunch, don't forget, and then we're going up to the mine to explore."

I gave them a thumbs-up and followed Logan around the shed to the parking lot. He was looking at me strangely as we walked back through the lodge to the game room. Teresa and Rachel were reading the printouts, frowns on both of their faces. Teresa put the pages back down on the table as we walked in. "Are you serious?" She looked at each of us in turn, with a gulp and a slight shudder. "This really happened out in the woods this morning?"

I didn't say anything, just plopped down into an easy chair. Logan nodded as he plopped down on the couch next to her. "Any doubts I may have had before, I don't have anymore." He ran his hand through his hair. "It was pretty fucking freaky, to be honest. I don't think I've ever been so scared in my life."

"Are you okay?" Rachel asked me with a slight shiver. "But I'm not sorry I wasn't with you guys." She shivered again, hugging herself. "I suppose all three of you could just be fucking with us, but"—she grinned—"you aren't smart enough to come up with something this elaborate."

"I'm not sure whether to be flattered or insulted," Logan replied, crossing his eyes as he scratched his head.

"Flattered, of course," Rachel batted her eyes at him with a ridiculous smile on her face. "I would never say anything insulting to you."

He rolled his eyes. "So what did you girls find out in town?"

"So glad you asked—you guys aren't going to believe this." Teresa opened her shoulder bag and pulled out a sheaf of papers. "Like Miss Tyler said yesterday, poor Albert's murder was one of the biggest things to happen in North Hollow—at least up to that point." She made a face. "Anyone who thinks the tabloids are bad today—they got nothing on the way real newspapers were back then. The *North Hollow Times* pretty much tried and convicted Robert Shelby the minute they found Albert's body." She glanced over at Rachel, who gave her a slight nod. She passed us each a photocopy without a word.

When I looked down at it, my blood ran cold.

It was a photograph, grainy and that same sepia tone as the ones at the historical society. It looked like—

Me.

And the caption underneath read "Pervert Robert Shelby: Wanted for the Murder of Albert Tyler."

I swallowed. *"Pervert?"*

"The paper wouldn't say exactly what they meant by that, but apparently Shelby had been run out of Boston for 'perversions'— sometimes they called it 'crimes against nature'—they found that out after the murder, of course." Teresa swallowed. "The resemblance is uncanny, isn't it? And I think we can be pretty sure what they meant by perversions and crimes against nature, can't we?"

My head was spinning. I couldn't take my eyes off the sepia-toned image.

Like the one of Albert, it looked enough like me for the two of us to be twins. Yes, the hair was different, and there was a scar on his cheek, but the resemblance...if Albert and Robert stood next to each other, and I with Marc...

"So Albert looked like your boyfriend, and Robert looked like you," Carson said in the silence. "I guess that kind of explains why Albert's ghost felt compelled to try to communicate with you."

"I'm not sure it's Albert, after all," I said slowly, unable to take my eyes away from the picture. "We've thought so, from the very beginning, because this all started at Albert's grave, and we hear the voice calling Bertie. But what if it's *Robert's* ghost?"

No one said anything, and when I looked up, they were all staring at me.

"I *see* Albert," I went on, my voice quiet and low. "If I was getting flashes of memory from Albert, I wouldn't see him, would I? I have no proof, of course, other than this"—I tapped the picture with my index finger—"but come on. Robert looks like me, Albert looks like *Marc*. Marc and I—we're a couple. According to this, Robert was gay—and the *feelings* I have—whenever I see Albert I feel the same way I do when I see Marc. I think Robert was in love with Albert—"

"And he killed him?" Teresa's voice was hushed. "Oh my God, that's so horrible."

"You guys said the time I passed out I kept saying *not dead, not dead, not dead*," I went on, not willing to stop to think any more about it. I wanted to say it, get it out there. If I was wrong, so be it, but I knew, somehow I knew deep inside I wasn't. "Maybe it was an accident. Maybe Robert killed him and it was an accident."

"Not dead," Carson said, stroking his chin. "Something someone might say if they killed someone by accident—you're not dead, not dead, you can't be dead, no you can't be dead—yeah, that makes sort of sense."

"And maybe Albert is calling him," I finished. "Sure, the most common nickname for Robert is Rob or Bob or Bobby—but it could also be Bertie. Ro-*bert*."

"Wow." Rachel got up. "I don't even know what to say to that, Scotty. It makes sense…but…" She walked over to the computer and sat down. She started typing, her fingers flying over the keyboard. "Teresa and I also came up with a theory. You know, it's possible we might be completely off-base about all of this, and have been from the very start," she said, biting her lower lip. "Did it ever occur to you that this might be past-life experiences instead of ghosts?"

Everyone turned to stare at her.

She turned sideways in the chair so she could face us all. "Outside of that first night in the cemetery, what has happened that could be explained as a haunting? I mean, really. Doesn't it make more sense that Scotty is having flashes of a past life, lived up here?" She smiled triumphantly at us. "And even the cemetery—couldn't what Scotty experienced in there be explained away as a natural occurrence when the wall in his mind between this life and the past life was breached?"

For once, Carson was at a loss for words. His mouth opened and closed a few times, but no sound came out.

Rachel's smile was rather self-satisfied. "You're not the only one in this family with a brain." She turned back to the computer and clicked a few keys. The printer hummed and started spitting out pages.

I kept staring at the picture in my hands. It might have been a picture of me taken at one of those photo studios they always have in amusement parks, where you can dress in period costumes and they take your picture, processing it so it looks like it was taken in that time. It was possible, I supposed, that it was all taking place in my head.

It was Logan who finally broke the silence by saying, "That doesn't explain what happened to us in the woods this morning."

Carson blew out his breath. "Yes, that is very true." He looked and sounded relieved that Rachel was wrong.

"Collective hallucinations?" Rachel asked, frowning. She let out a sigh.

"No, I don't think so," Logan said with a shudder. "If that was a hallucination—no way, man. No offense, girls, it's a great theory, and I'd be more likely to believe that than the ghost story—if I hadn't experienced it myself. And Scotty's mom heard the voice, didn't she? There's no way that was a collective hallucination." He frowned.

They kept talking, but I tuned them out. It wasn't an intellectual exercise for me anymore. I *knew*. They'd been in love, I thought as I stared at the picture that could have been a sepia mirror. In love, and a terrible tragedy had happened.

That was the sadness I kept feeling.

But still—even my own theory had an enormous hole in it.

Robert Shelby had run away. He hadn't died here, the way Albert had. So there was no reason for him to be haunting the mountainside.

But how was I seeing Albert? How was that possible?

I reached for the prints of microfiche the girls had made of the newspapers at the library. I looked over the pages, my heart aching with each horrible article I read about the search for Robert Shelby. It was all the same thing, really—sensationalist reporting of the shocking murder of poor young Albert Tyler. Clearly, the angle the editor of the paper had decided to go for was that Albert was practically a saint in his absolute perfection. Everyone who knew him loved him and was certain he was destined for a great future, his loss was a loss to not just his friends and family but the world and society, blah, blah, blah. I'm sure the Tylers had been thrilled to read such laudatory articles about their youngest son, but I found it hard to believe that anyone was so perfect. I certainly wasn't, and neither was anyone I knew.

And there was nothing too vile for the reporters to say about Robert Shelby, who was unable to defend himself. They never mentioned what the perversions or what the crimes against nature were that got him run out of Boston—and even mentioned several times that they couldn't "because it was a family paper"—but they made it very clear that the Bostonians should have killed him rather than settling for chasing him away, leaving him alive to spread his sick perversions to another community. An editorial even said, "If only the good people of Boston had done their proper duty by their fellow citizens, young Albert's light would not have been extinguished so young."

It was pretty clear to me the girls had been right about what exactly the perversion was—he was gay in a time when homosexuality was a mental disorder as well as a crime. He had been lucky to get out of Boston alive—there was a quote from someone high up in the Boston police department: *I felt as though we should have taken more action against Mr. Shelby besides ordering him to leave town, as he was clearly unrepentant, almost defiant, about his crimes here in Boston. I was certain he was going to infect another community somewhere, but it wasn't my decision to make, and he left Boston in the middle of the night to escape any further judgment against him, and I reckoned it was up to God to punish him. My heart breaks for that poor family.*

And I knew the next gay man in Boston who had run afoul of the police didn't escape with his life—not after this happened.

I felt sick to my stomach.

Thank God times have changed—things still need to get better but at least this kind of thing doesn't happen anymore.

"Robert didn't kill Albert," I said. "I just know it."

"That could explain why both of them are still here, on this plane, unable to cross over to the other side," Carson replied. "Albert needs for the truth to come out, and Robert needs to have his name cleared." He frowned. "But Robert got away, didn't he? If they'd have lynched him, they would have been really proud of killing a monster—they wouldn't have hidden it, would they?"

"Maybe what we felt in the woods today—maybe that was the real killer," Logan suggested. He sat on the overstuffed arm of my chair and slapped my thigh with his hand. "But I don't understand why this is all just happening now, and it hasn't before." He flushed a bit. "I asked Annie"—he gave me a sidelong glance, as though to say *don't say a word about what you saw*—"and she had no idea, said there's never been any reports of ghosts or anything." He blushed even darker. "She kind of thought I was a little crazy for even bringing it up, so I had to change the subject pretty fast."

"Did you sacrifice your chance of getting into her pants?" Rachel spun around in the chair.

Logan made a face at her, and it occurred to me for the first time that I wasn't the only person in our group that found him attractive.

Before he could say anything to her, Carson said, "It is curious, isn't it?" He turned to me and smiled. "It's like *your* presence here is what triggered it all, Scotty."

"And the trip to the cemetery," Rachel added. "If we hadn't gone to the cemetery, maybe none of this would have happened."

"Maybe, maybe not." Carson ignored the snarkiness in her voice and treated her question seriously. "I guess we'll never know— but I do think the restless spirit would have connected with Scotty anyway. Going to the cemetery just made it easier." He cleared his throat. "I'm thinking we might need to try to communicate directly with Albert's spirit."

"And how do you propose we do that?" This from Teresa, looking up from the papers she was reading.

"A séance."

"Don't we need a medium for that?" Rachel replied. She smirked at him. "I may not have interned at the show, but I do watch it."

"No," I said slowly. "We don't need one. We can do it ourselves." I took a deep breath. "I vote we do it tonight."

CHAPTER TWELVE

For the rest of the day, tension seemed to just build with every passing hour.

I didn't think the day would ever end.

Minutes crept by, and constantly checking my watch or any clock in the nearby vicinity didn't help matters. I'd never known time to move so slowly, and with each tick of a passing second my nerves got worse. I kept swinging emotionally from wanting to get it all over with and being afraid we were messing with things we shouldn't be messing with.

It's not like Carson was an expert on the supernatural by any means. Who knew what could happen? So many things could go wrong...and I had a strong sense that something bad *was* going to happen.

It was like sitting in the dentist's outer office and hearing the drill making that horrible buzzing sound, and knowing soon enough I'd be the one in the chair with my head tilted back and the drill in my mouth, the smell of burning teeth nauseating me as the drill dug rot out.

My mom always said that worrying was like borrowing trouble.

But I could talk myself down from the panic. The anticipation of the drill was, after all, much worse than the actual experience. And even though I knew there was something that wanted to harm me, I somehow knew that it wasn't Robert or Albert or whichever one of them it was who'd been invading my mind. They were benign, they wanted to help save me from whatever dark force it was out there in the woods.

The dark force was what was to be feared. And I had to believe it couldn't really hurt me, despite the evil intent I'd felt from it in the woods.

It has to be the killer, the one who really killed Albert, I reassured myself. *That's why Albert can't rest—he knows Robert was innocent.*

These thoughts slowed my heart rate down and helped the fear to pass, which was better, but the calm soon turned again to impatience.

Going to the garnet mine now seemed like a good idea—I figured it was a distraction, and I certainly could use something to take my mind off what was going to happen that night. The other option was to hang around the lodge by myself—which certainly would have been much, much worse.

The garnet mine probably *would* have been interesting on any other day or any other vacation, but as we walked through and the guide lectured us on the finer points of garnet mining and its history in the region, my mind just kept wandering. I tried to get interested in what she was telling us—we were the only people in the group—but she just didn't hold my attention. I kept thinking about Marc. Once we'd been led into the mine I wanted to distract myself from my fears and worries, and what better way to do that than thinking about my boyfriend? But it actually had the opposite effect—my mind seemed to transfer my worries about tonight into worries about Marc.

And it didn't take long for the worry to turn into fear.

His dad is so crazy, maybe there's another level of meaning to his texts and maybe—maybe there's a reason why his dad took their phones. Maybe he's finally completely lost it. Maybe they're in danger. Maybe that's what this whole thing is about—maybe Albert is trying to warn me that Marc's in danger, that he's going to be killed...

"Stop that, stop freaking yourself out," I told myself sternly.

I gave my attention back to the tour guide. I suppose it was interesting—Teresa and Rachel certainly looked fascinated, like they were hanging on the guide's every word—but I just couldn't make myself care. I hadn't dressed warmly enough, either. It was chilly inside the mine, and I couldn't wait for us to get out of there. But of course, after the tour was finished, we had to go to the gift shop, where the girls picked out garnet jewelry for themselves, even though they could never seem to make up their minds on any particular piece. Our mothers were no better, and finally, in disgust, I went back outside.

The gift shop was on another plateau of the mountain, with a huge lawn of perfectly trimmed and edged grass and flowerbeds. At the far end of the lawn, the forest began again, on the other side of a barbed-wire fence. After the cool of the inside of the mine and the air conditioning in the gift shop, it felt warm outside, so I sat down in the grass next to the driveway where the cars were parked and pulled out my phone—there was signal here, hooray—and scrolled through my e-mails. I started writing out texts to Marc maybe three or four times, but every time deleted them without hitting send. Carson and Logan wandered across the lawn to the fence. I saw them talking animatedly, but when they wandered back and I asked them about it they both claimed it was nothing.

I didn't believe them, and that just made me even more uneasy than I already was.

By the time the women were through in the gift shop, it was past six. Rather than going back to the lodge for dinner we went to a restaurant on the state highway. With all eleven of us clustered around an enormous table, talking and joking and laughing, my unease continued to grow—especially as the light began to fade from the sky outside the restaurant's windows.

It's not too late to change your mind you don't have to do this.

But I didn't really believe that was true.

There was a certain inevitability about the séance, about trying to reach Albert, I couldn't deny—whether I wanted to or not.

Just because you don't want to try to reach Albert doesn't mean he won't try to reach you. And you can't control that. You've never had any control. The séance, at least, is trying to take some control over these happenings.

I got a text from Marc right after the entrées arrived. I excused myself from the table—getting an odd look from Carson when I did—and slipped away to answer it while everyone dug into their dinner. I didn't want my lobster mac-and-cheese to get cold, and I could have answered the text at the table, but I just wanted some privacy with Marc—even if it was really just a stupid text message.

His text simply said, *Miss you and wish you were back already. Will Sunday ever come?*

Tears filled my eyes as I read it again. I walked around to the back of the restaurant and sat down, and let the tears come. I allowed myself to just sob—and as I cried the tension and stress of the day seemed to ease up a bit. I wiped at my eyes and got control of myself. I'd needed to release some of the pressure, and now I felt a lot better, more in control of myself.

The sun was getting low in the west—it was now after eight—and I typed out quickly, *Is everything okay with you?* Within a minute I got a response, *Dad's been rough but other than that okay. Just wish you were here.*

I couldn't shake the sense that something was terribly wrong back home, but I wrote it off as nerves. I was all keyed up and needed to get a grip.

But as it drew closer, I was becoming more and more worried about the séance.

I'd agreed to do it because I wanted the whole thing to be over and hoped that communicating directly with whatever spirit was haunting me might finally do the trick. Maybe things had been hard because I'd blocked myself, resisted out of fear, I don't know. At the time, it seemed like the right way to go to get it over and done with, so maybe I could enjoy the rest of my vacation—so we all could, really. And the parents were starting to suspect something was going on with us. My mother had cornered me outside the garnet mine gift shop and quizzed me thoroughly, but I'd managed to fend off most of her questions and satisfy her. I'd noticed Nancy Stark cornered Logan in the mine, and they'd had a quickly whispered conversation—likewise Lynda Wolfe with Rachel.

But we hadn't had a chance to compare notes with each other. I went back inside and slid back into my seat, giving everyone a brittle smile. My lobster mac-and-cheese was still steaming. "Everything okay?" Logan asked as I picked up my spoon. I smiled and nodded. The table had fallen silent when I came back, but as soon as I sat down everyone started talking again. As I ate, I couldn't help watching as the night sky grew darker and darker outside the windows. "Got somewhere to be, son?" my dad asked with a big grin on his face as I checked my watch again.

I smiled back at him. "No, Dad, I—"

Carson cut me off quickly. "Uncle Hank, we were thinking about going for a walk later, down by the lake." He gave me a weird look that was clearly meant as a warning for me to keep my mouth shut.

Because *of course* I was going to tell my father and all the other adults in our group that we were planning on having a séance and contacting a spirit.

I just shook my head at him.

But finally, dinner was over and the check paid and we were all heading back up the mountain road in our respective cars. I didn't hear from Marc again—I didn't expect to, frankly—and it seemed to take another eternity before the parents were back in the lodge's bar area with a couple of bottles of wine and the Trivial Pursuit game.

"You kids be careful," Jerry Stark yelled after us as we walked out of the lodge. "No going in the water."

"Like we would," Rachel muttered.

"So, where are we going to do this?" I asked. My nerves were jittery, and I could hear my voice shaking just a little bit. "I thought we were going to do it in the game room."

Carson shook his head and pulled a flashlight out of the backpack he'd been carrying around all day. He turned it on and pointed it at the woods. "I think it would work better down at the ruins," he said, not looking at me.

The ruins?

My heart sank and my stomach knotted. "I don't know—"

"It makes sense," Rachel interrupted me softly. She took my hand. "We talked about it this afternoon—we're all scared, too, Scotty, but it makes the most sense. The ruins—that seems to be the heart of where this is all coming from. And if we're all together, we should be safe, right?"

"You don't know that," I replied, but somehow, I sensed she was right. I'd known, somehow, all along, that the cabin was the key.

Carson led us into the forest single file. The wind was moving through the trees above our heads, branches swaying gently as we walked down the path. I felt oddly calm. The night was silent other than the whispering breeze. I allowed my mind to wander, not wanting to think about what might lie ahead for me and the others. There was a little part of me that kept thinking we were making a huge mistake, we were playing with powers far beyond our comprehension. I almost felt like I was making my last walk, that the path was actually leading me to a public execution.

Grim thoughts.

When we reached the cabin, Carson handed the flashlight over to Logan and pulled a big woolen blanket out of his backpack, which he spread on the ground. We all took seats in a circle, and he then lit an enormous candle, which he set in the middle. We joined hands.

Carson began talking in a low voice. "Tonight, we come seeking the spirit who has haunted these woods, with light from the world of the living to the world of the spirit. We mean you no harm—we merely want to get some answers from you..."

He kept talking, and even with my eyes closed, I could tell things were changing. The wind was picking up, and I could feel it blowing my hair around. Yet the candle continued to burn as Carson's voice got louder.

And I felt it coming, whatever it was, I knew it—I could feel it as the hairs on my arm and the back of my neck stood up. I wanted to scream, to get up and run as far as I could, not stop running until I got to the airport in Albany, get on a plane and just keep moving because anything would be better than this, this horrible sense of something awful about to happen, but I couldn't stop it, I couldn't control it, I was completely helpless...

And it started.

Whatever or whomever it was, it started with a prickling feeling at the back of my head, like it was probing my brain, trying to find a way inside. I was terrified, positively terrified, but there was nothing I could do, I'd agreed to this and had to see it through. So I took a deep breath and let go of myself.

And it was like it poured into me, and I could sense its joy, its relief, at finally finding a vessel. Rachel's hand on my right tightened, squeezing really hard, and I heard someone gasp, but it wasn't something I felt like I needed to focus on as I was being filled up with whatever—

—Albert, it is I, Albert—

—and I opened my eyes.

I heard Carson asking something but his voice sounded so far away, like we were on a phone call with a really bad connection. I could see him, too, his face shadowed in the flickering candlelight, and I heard myself answering but it wasn't my voice. But I didn't feel afraid because somehow, somehow I felt reassured because I knew Albert didn't want to hurt me, he wanted to help me and he wanted us to help him somehow but I didn't know how—

—and the dark began to fade as the clearing began to fill with light again, and I could see the trees again, and it was the same as it was all those years ago.

When the tragedy happened.

Shhhh, Albert whispered inside of my brain, *watch and listen. You know it's important. You understand, don't you?*

And I saw it all, like I was there.

But I *was* there, in a way. It was warm, spring, with just a slight hint of chill in the air. I could hear the sound of trickling water. The rose blooms were ready to open on the bushes planted just the year before, when the cabin had been finished and Robert, sweet Robert, had moved in.

And Robert was there, lowering the bucket into the well. His hair—so much like mine, thick and curly and black, hanging down to his shoulders but pulled back and tied with a piece of fabric to keep it out of his face. His broad shoulders stretching the fabric of his shirt, which was damp with sweat under the arms and in the center of the back. He was also barefoot, and he took a drink of the cool, clean water and sighed in pleasure.

"Robert!"

I turned and could see him, Albert, coming down the path, the look of concern on his face, as he brushed his reddish-gold hair out of his own eyes. He was hurrying, almost running, and he was slightly out of breath.

"Go away, Albert, go back to your girl," Robert said, letting go of the bucket and turning away from the well. His voice sounded tired rather than angry, resigned. "I don't want to be a part of this anymore."

"Robert!" His voice cracked in despair and sadness, and Robert stopped walking. "I love you, you know that. I want us to be together when we go to the city—"

"What would be the point?" Robert's voice sounded weary, and I could sense how tired and broken he was. He'd been run out of Boston for loving another boy, accused of all kinds of things, and he'd come here to collect himself and put his life back together, to deny the urges that got him into trouble out in Boston and find a woman, live a decent life.

He hadn't counted on finding Albert, his Bertie, and falling in love all over again.

He loves me, he does, Bertie whispered to me inside my head, *and I love him.*

"I'm sorry," Albert whispered. "But I kissed her—I kissed her for us."

Robert turned and looked back, his pain written all over his face. "For us?" He half smiled. "And how do you figure that, my Bertie?"

And when I heard him say the word *Bertie,* I knew. I recognized the voice I'd heard, even though it had sounded empty and hollow as the word had swirled through the woods at night. I'd been wrong, so wrong, Bertie was Albert and Robert was calling him, still calling for him, all these years later.

"He knows, Robbie." Bertie's voice cracked. "He suspects. I know he's written to Boston about you—about why you left, he saw something—"

The words affected Robert, the color draining out of his face, and he swayed on his feet, reaching out and touching the brick base of the well so he didn't fall.

"No," he whispered. "How—how can it be?"

"Molly told him," Albert's face twisted in a sneer. "She suspects—and she's jealous and angry. That was why I kissed her, Robbie. I need to convince her she's wrong, that there's nothing between you and me." His voice broke again. "If I have to spend the summer making love to her to protect you, so be it, Robert, I will do it. I will do whatever I have to do to make sure that nothing ever happens to you. I love you."

Robert held out his hand, and Albert took it, pressing it to his lips.

Then I felt it.

The darkness, the evil, was coming like a shadow over the sun.

And it was dangerous, consumed with fury and anger, so consumed with the rage it was close to crossing the line into madness.

It was terrifying.

I wanted to scream at them to run, but there was nothing I could do. *Watch,* the voice said inside my head again, *watch so you will understand and you will know what you have to do.*

I turned and saw the man, and my heart lurched.

If Robert looked like me, and Albert like Marc, the man on the path carrying the shovel was a dead ringer for Mr. Krueger.

My stomach twisted into a knot of horror.

But somehow, I'd always known.

He was a big man, thickly built from hard work cutting down trees and swinging an ax or a hammer. His arms were thick, his shoulders were thick, and so was his neck. I'd never realized before just how big Mr. Krueger was. He was wearing suspenders holding up his black wool trousers and a red and black flannel shirt, and his face was twisted in anger and rage.

"Take your foul sinner's hands off my son!" he shouted, and frightened birds took off in droves from the trees around the clearing. Robert and Albert sprang apart.

"I wanted to believe the little slut was a liar," he went on as he came into the clearing, his grip on the shovel with his left hand tightening so that his knuckles turned white. "I didn't want to believe that any son of mine could be so twisted, so sick, so perverted. But here you are, with your arms around a man, acting like a woman. Is that what I raised, another girl child?"

Albert stepped forward, his chin going up in the air. "Papa, it's not what you think—it's not a sin. I love him."

The slap sent Albert sprawling on his back, and Robert stepped forward, in between the son and his angry father.

"Don't hurt him," Robert said softly. "I am to blame. Don't punish him for the sin I led him into."

Albert was getting to his feet as his father lifted the shovel and swung it.

The sound of Robert's skull cracking echoed through the woods as his body went down, a trickle of blood coming out of his mouth.

"He's not dead," Albert said, almost drunkenly, his face white in shock as he staggered over to where Robert's lifeless body lay. "No, he can't be dead, I don't believe it. He's not dead."

And he looked up at his father, his face twisted in hatred. "Murderer! You'll hang for this!" He got to his feet. "If it's the last thing I do, I'll see you hang! I hate you! I hate you!"

And then his face changed, and he ran. He ran through the bushes, down the path heading to where the beaver pond was, running as quickly as he could, terrified because he knew now that his father had crossed the line, had gone completely insane, and was going to kill him, he was no longer his father's son but some kind of monster that needed to be destroyed, and so he ran, his heart in his throat even as he sobbed while he ran, the shock and horror that Robert was dead, his father had killed Robert and he hated, oh, how he hated.

He stumbled and fell, and looked up to see his father, carrying the shovel stained with Robert's blood, the evil glint in his father's eyes as he raised the shovel and brought it down on his son's head.

Bertie.

And as his body died, as his soul separated from his flesh, he saw Robert, on the other bank. And then he faded away.

And the light began to fade and I felt Albert slipping away from me, slipping away from me like he was dying all over again, a hundred and six years later he was dying again, and as my eyes began to focus and I could see the flame of the candle, and I knew I was weeping, there were tears coming out of my eyes, and I knew—I knew as surely as I knew my name was Scotty Thompson, I knew what this had all been about, all along, there had always been more going on here just as Carson had suspected, but we'd always been wrong.

And I blinked, and he was gone from my mind as if he'd never been there, and I let go of Rachel's and Teresa's hands and wiped at my eyes.

"Mr. Tyler killed them both," I said as they all stared at me, their eyes wide open and their faces pale. "I don't understand it all, I don't understand how it works, the spirit world or whatever you want to call it, but they've been waiting all these years." I turned and looked at the well. "Mr. Tyler threw Robert's body down the well, along with the shovel he used to kill them both. He wrecked the well so no one would ever know that was really where Robert Shelby was. He lied and spent the rest of his life making sure that in death they remained apart. They truly loved each other."

I got up and grabbed the flashlight and walked over to the well. I picked up a rock and smashed away at the rotting boards a murderer had used to seal the well. Once the hole was big enough, I pointed the flashlight down the well.

And there, on the dried bottom, a skull grinned back up at me.

I turned to the others. "I think we now know what Albert wanted us to know, all along."

I felt an enormous relief, like the forest emitted a big sigh.

And it seemed, out of the corner of my eye, I saw them again—Albert and Robert—putting their arms around each other.

You know what you have to do.

I got up and ran away from the clearing. I could hear the others calling after me, but I couldn't stop. I had to get back to the lodge, back to the game room where the Wi-Fi was so my phone would work.

Marc was in danger.

That was what it had all been about, from the very beginning.

History repeating itself.

His father took his phone. His father's crazy, he always has been, there's always been something wrong with him.

I remembered the joy I'd felt that first night in the cemetery and now knew it for what it was—joy and relief that finally the cycle could be broken, that I was there and the two of them somehow could reach me.

My emotions were out of control as I reached the fork in the trail and turned toward the lodge. I could hear the others coming after me as I reached into my pocket and pulled out my phone. I kept running, tears running down the side of my face.

In my head I was getting flashes of it.

I was inside the Krueger house. I could smell something cooking—lasagna, maybe, and garlic. I saw him sitting at his worktable in the basement. Marc's phone was there, open and on, and I could see text messages. I could see the anger and fury and madness in Mr. Krueger's eyes as he opened the desk drawer and pulled out a gun, checking the chamber for bullets.

I ran faster, my lungs contracting and tears streaming out of my eyes, a pain stabbing through me in the side, but I couldn't stop running, I had to be able to get Marc on the phone and warn him to get out of the house—

Mr. Krueger was climbing the stairs, the gun in his hand.

I burst out of the woods and ran across the parking lot. I pulled open the door and saw Annie Bartlett staring as I ran across the carpet. I heard my mother call my name, but I ignored her as I saw the blessed bars finally show up on my screen.

I stopped, gasping for air, as I pulled up Marc's entry in my address book. Sweat and tears rolled down the sides of my face as my trembling finger pushed his home number, and I slapped the phone to the side of my face.

Marc answered on the third ring. "Hello?"

"Marc—" I could barely talk, I was breathing so hard. I tried to catch my breath, form the words.

"Scotty? Are you all right?"

"You...need to get out of the house, now!"

"Dad?" There was a clatter as the phone dropped, and I could hear everything in the background.

"No!" I heard Mrs. Krueger scream.

I heard a gunshot and sank to my knees.

A scream.

My entire body went numb.

I felt a hand on my shoulder.

"Scotty?'" Marc said.

"Marc?"

He sounded strange. "I have to hang up." His voice was weirdly monosyllabic. "My dad...my mom...he was going to kill me..."

"What happened?"

"Have to call 911."

The call was disconnected.

"Is he okay?" Teresa asked.

I looked up at my friends. Their faces were white, their eyes wide.

I nodded.

And everything went black.

EPILOGUE

The airport in Albany was a small one, with only a few gates, so despite the fact we were all going in different directions we were able to sit together until the flights started boarding.

"It'll be okay." Rachel gave me a kiss on the cheek. "Marc and his mom will be fine, you'll see."

Mrs. Krueger had gotten between her husband and her son when he'd come upstairs with the gun, murder on his mind. She'd fought him for the gun, and it had gone off, killing him. She hadn't been charged with anything yet, Marc had told me, but he felt guilty. He was blaming himself for everything, no matter how much I'd tried to explain to him it wasn't his fault.

But it was hard to do over the phone or through text messages. I hoped I could make him understand everything better face to face.

I hoped.

They called our flight, and my parents moved toward the gate to board.

I turned to my friends for one last good-bye.

Since the séance, the week had been kind of crazy.

The discovery of the skeleton had been a bit of a nine days' wonder in North Hollow. We'd been interviewed by the police, of course, and they'd found a waterproof satchel with the whole skeleton down there.

It was Robert Shelby.

I hugged everyone in turn and said good-bye.

"Tell Marc we can't wait to meet him," Teresa whispered in my ear.

"I will." I smiled back at her.

Carson walked with me to the gate. We hugged one last time, and I said, "You know, there's something I've been meaning to ask you."

He raised his eyebrows.

"I mean, I get it—you know, that Albert was tied to the place because he died violently, and had the time to hate his father…but Robert? Why was Robert still there, calling for Albert? I mean, he died violently, but…"

Carson took his glasses off and rubbed them with his T-shirt. He cleared his throat. "I don't pretend to know all the answers, Scotty… and my theory is kind of, I don't know, kind of sentimental." He put his glasses back on. "But how could Robert rest as long as Albert wasn't?" His eyes filled with tears. "If it was you, and it was Marc, could you? Or would you spend however long it took, calling him? Wanting him to come with you?"

I wiped at my own eyes and hugged him.

I boarded the plane.

Rest in peace, Albert and Robert.

About the Author

Greg Herren is a New Orleans-based author and editor. Former editor of *Lambda Book Report*, he is also a co-founder of the Saints and Sinners Literary Festival, which takes place in New Orleans every May. He is the author of ten novels, including the Lambda Literary Award winning *Murder in the Rue Chartres*, called by the *New Orleans Times-Picayune* "the most honest depiction of life in post-Katrina New Orleans published thus far." He co-edited *Love, Bourbon Street: Reflections on New Orleans*, which also won the Lambda Literary Award. He has published over fifty short stories in markets as varied as *Ellery Queen's Mystery Magazine* to the critically acclaimed anthology *New Orleans Noir* to various websites, literary magazines, and anthologies.

A long-time resident of New Orleans, Greg was a fitness columnist and book reviewer for Window Media for over four years, publishing in the LGBT newspapers *IMPACT News*, *Southern Voice*, and *Houston Voice*. He served a term on the Board of Directors for the National Stonewall Democrats, and served on the founding committee of the Louisiana Stonewall Democrats. He is currently employed as a public health researcher for the NO/AIDS Task Force.

Soliloquy Titles From Bold Strokes Books

Lake Thirteen by Greg Herren. A visit to an old cemetery seems like fun to a group of five teenagers, who soon learn that sometimes it's best to leave old ghosts alone. (978-1-60282-894-0)

The Road to Her by KE Payne. Sparks fly when actress Holly Croft, star of UK soap Portobello Road, meets her new on-screen love interest, the enigmatic and sexy Elise Manford. (978-1-60282-887-2)

Kings of Ruin by Sam Cameron. High school student Danny Kelly and loner Kevin Clark must team up to defeat a top-secret alien intelligence that likes to wreak havoc with fiery car, truck, and train accidents. (978-1-60282-864-3)

Swans & Klons by Nora Olsen. In a future world where there are no males, sixteen-year-old Rubric and her girlfriend Salmon Jo must fight to survive when everything they believed in turns out to be a lie. (978-1-60282-874-2)

The You Know Who Girls by Annameekee Hesik. As they begin freshman year, Abbey Brooks and her best friend, Kate, pinky swear they'll keep away from the lesbians in Gila High, but Abbey already suspects she's one of those you-know-who girls herself and slowly learns who her true friends really are. (978-1-60282-754-7)

In Stone by Jeremy Jordan King. A young New Yorker is rescued from a hate crime by a mysterious someone who turns out to be more of a something. (978-1-60282-761-5)

Wonderland by David-Matthew Barnes. After her mother's sudden death, Destiny Moore is sent to live with her two gay uncles on Avalon Cove, a mysterious island on which she uncovers a secret place called Wonderland, where love and magic prove to be real. (978-1-60282-788-2)

Another 365 Days by KE Payne. Clemmie Atkins is back, and her life is more complicated than ever! Still madly in love with her girlfriend, Clemmie suddenly finds her life turned upside down with distractions, confessions, and the return of a familiar face... (978-1-60282-775-2)

The Secret of Othello by Sam Cameron. Florida teen detectives Steven and Denny risk their lives to search for a sunken NASA satellite—but under the waves, no one can hear you scream... (978-1-60282-742-4)

Andy Squared by Jennifer Lavoie. Andrew never thought anyone could come between him and his twin sister, Andrea...until Ryder rode into town. (978-1-60282-743-1)

Sara by Greg Herren. A mysterious and beautiful new student at Southern Heights High School stirs things up when students start dying. (978-1-60282-674-8)

Boys of Summer, edited by Steve Berman. Stories of young love and adventure, when the sky's ceiling is a bright blue marvel, when another boy's laughter at the beach can distract from dull summer jobs. (978-1-60282-663-2)

Street Dreams by Tama Wise. Tyson Rua has more than his fair share of problems growing up in New Zealand—he's gay, he's falling in love, and he's run afoul of the local hip-hop crew leader just as he's trying to make it as a graffiti artist. (978-1-60282-650-2)

me@you.com by KE Payne. Is it possible to fall in love with someone you've never met? Imogen Summers thinks so because it's happened to her. (978-1-60282-592-5)

Swimming to Chicago by David-Matthew Barnes. As the lives of the adults around them unravel, high school students Alex and Robby form an unbreakable bond, vowing to do anything to stay together—even if it means leaving everything behind. (978-1-60282-572-7)

365 Days by KE Payne. Life sucks when you're seventeen years old and confused about your sexuality, and the girl of your dreams doesn't even know you exist. Then in walks sexy new emo girl, Hannah Harrison. Clemmie Atkins has exactly 365 days to discover herself, and she's going to have a blast doing it! (978-1-60282-540-6)

Cursebusters! by Julie Smith. Budding psychic Reeno is the most accomplished teenage burglar in California, but one tiny screw-up and poof!—she's sentenced to Bad Girl School. And that isn't even her worst problem. Her sister Haley's dying of an illness no one can diagnose, and now she can't even help. (978-1-60282-559-8)

Who I Am by M.L. Rice. Devin Kelly's senior year is a disaster. She's in a new school in a new town, and the school bully is making her life miserable—but then she meets his sister Melanie and realizes her feelings for her are more than platonic. (978-1-60282-231-3)

Sleeping Angel by Greg Herren. Eric Matthews survives a terrible car accident only to find out everyone in town thinks he's a murderer—and he has to clear his name even though he has no memories of what happened. (978-1-60282-214-6)

Mesmerized by David-Matthew Barnes. Through her close friendship with Brodie and Lance, Serena Albright learns about the many forms of love and finds comfort for the grief and guilt she feels over the brutal death of her older brother, the victim of a hate crime. (978-1-60282-191-0)